A Shadow on the Wall

Dale T. Phillips

Thanks for being a reader
Dale

Copyright © 2015 Genretarium Publishing

First printing, 2013, Rosstrum Publishing

135798642

Cover Design copyright 2013-2015 Melinda Phillips
http://www.snapichic.com

ISBN: 0692433147
ISBN-13: 978-0692433140

Try these other works by Dale T. Phillips

Shadow of the Wendigo (Supernatural Thriller)

The Zack Taylor Mystery Series
A Memory of Grief
A Fall From Grace
A Shadow on the Wall

Story Collections
Fables and Fantasies (Fantasy)
Crooked Paths (Mystery/Crime)
Strange Tales (Magic Realism, Paranormal)
Apocalypse Tango (Science Fiction)
Halls of Horror (Horror)
Jumble Sale (Mixed Genres)
The Big Book of Genre Stories (Different Genres)

Non-fiction Career Help
How to Improve Your Interviewing Skills

With Other Authors
Insanity Tales
Rogue Wave: Best New England Crime Stories 2015

Sign up for my newsletter to get special offers
http://www.daletphillips.com

DEDICATION

To John D. and Travis, who showed the way for a flawed knight-errant

ACKNOWLEDGMENTS

While Zack is back, finally— a number of people have been asking for his next adventure, and here it is at last. It took a bit longer than expected, because I had more revision tasks to do— the results of a great editing staff, who were able to diligently shave away the fluff and tighten the language. A hearty thank you to Vlad Vaslyn, Joe Ross, Ursula Wong, and Pete Ewing— all authors in their own right, but who took the time and effort to read this work (multiple times) and offer their suggestions to make it better.

My thanks extend to everyone who helped to make this book possible. My first line of defense against writing that's not up to snuff is the Tyngsboro Writer's Group, including, but not limited to: Mike Johnson, Karen Johnson, Brian Hammar, and the Immortal Bernie Z. And thanks once again to the helpful staff at the Tyngsboro Public Library for giving us space to meet and work.

To Rosstrum Publishing, for bringing this book into being in the first edition, and to Genretarium Publishing, to give it renewed life.

To writers Pete Morin, Debbi Mack and David Daniel, all of whom have read a Zack Taylor book and allowed me to use their kind and generous words of praise. (Their books are great— buy them!)

As always, to my wonderful family: Mindy, Bridget, and Erin, for suffering my solitary profession of writing.

To my dear and supportive friends and loved ones for making things more enjoyable along the path of life.

To all those who have helped teach me to write, through their works.

To all those who read other Zack Taylor mysteries and wanted more.

And to you, dear reader, my thanks, for reading this one.

Feel free to contact me and let me know what you thought of the book and what it's about.

How can I be substantial if I do not cast a shadow? I must have a dark side also if I am to be whole.

—C.G. Jung

The abyss you stare into and that stares back at you is your reflection in the mirror - we all have it - that shadow self - that dark heart...

—John Geddes, A Familiar Rain

A shadow is hard to seize by the throat and dash to the ground.

—Victor Hugo, Les Misérables

CHAPTER 1

A grim-faced cop at your door always gives pause, even when it's someone you recognize. He emerged from the shadows at the top of the stairs, and stood there in a halo of light. He had something of import to tell me, and none of it could be good. Possibilities flashed through my mind in a rapid succession of horrors.

"Lieutenant McClaren," I said, when I could finally speak.

He nodded. "Tough day?"

"The absolute worst," I said, and swallowed. "Please do not give me any more bad news."

"Afraid I can't do that." I could hear apology in his voice. "This will make the rest of your day seem like the good part. We'd better go inside."

I lowered my head and slowly shook it, hoping he might go away if I pretended he wasn't there. He didn't move, didn't speak. Feeling like Sisyphus pushing his rock uphill, I climbed the remaining steps. I unlocked the door to my room, and he followed me inside.

I saw McClaren take in my Spartan accommodations with cop's eyes, starting with the efficiency kitchenette: refrigerator, stove, sink, and a table shimmed with a matchbook under one leg to keep it from wobbling. He tracked to the other side of the room, with only a bed, a nightstand, a very beat-up dresser, and a pile of books.

One eyebrow went up. "No TV?"

I shrugged.

He eyed the two mismatched chairs by the table. "Either of those actually hold any weight?"

"You can try it. No guarantees."

He frowned. "I'll skip. You really this broke?"

"I was, ah, living with someone. Things didn't work out."

"How long ago?"

"Few weeks."

"Uh-huh."

"What's that supposed to mean?"

He sighed. "It means you're still hoping to get back together, which is why you haven't got a real place instead of this shithole."

"Maybe I like squalor." I looked around now, and realized he was right. It still didn't mean I wanted to hear it. I was going to give him some lip, but I noticed his suit was rumpled, and his face was lined, his eyes lidded with fatigue. He was tall, tanned, and loose-limbed, more like a park ranger than a police lieutenant, but tonight all the crisp had gone out of him, as if the world had rolled him in an alley.

I spread my hands, palms up. "I've got so many problems right now, what's one more? Hit me."

McClaren's mouth turned down, like he was tasting something sour. "Ollie Southern's out."

Three little words. With the same effect as a doctor saying *Your cancer's back*.

"You okay?"

"No," I said. The air seemed to have gone out of me. "How'd he escape?"

"He didn't." McClaren rubbed his hand on his pant leg. "The feds got him cut loose."

"WHAT?"

"He turned snitch, ratted somebody else out, and they traded. They called the governor, who called a few people, who called us, and jolly Ollie went out free into the night."

All the strength of my legs gone, I slumped into a chair in the tiny kitchen space. "They just let him go? The guy and his gang get caught beating me to death, and they just let the sonofabitch go?"

"The feds have the clout. He's a little fish to them. He gives them a bigger one, they're happy to trade."

"Even if he comes back and kills me."

"Which he pretty much has to, after you got him sent there."

"I do not believe this." I ran my hand through my hair.

He looked around. "Got anything to drink?"

"No, I, uh, had a problem with it years ago. If I don't stay away from it, I'll drown in it."

McClaren nodded. "I know some cops like that."

"But not you."

He shook his head. "Just figured you could use a little something right now. So could I, tell you the truth. Some days I don't like my job very much. It burns me to nail these dirtbags and then have someone turn them loose."

"Getting caught red-handed means he should stay in."

"Yeah." McClaren paused, which seemed like an apology for the whole system. "Thought you should know."

"Thanks," I said. He'd come in person, and it hadn't been easy. I appreciated that it mattered to him.

"And I wish I didn't have to tell you this. But you've got to start looking over your shoulder. In fact, the best thing would be if you just left for someplace where he couldn't find you."

I gripped the tabletop. "You know why I came to Maine."

"To find the guys who killed your friend."

"Know why I stayed?"

"Why?"

"I've never put down roots before this, just spent my life running and hiding. I'm trying to change, to be responsible and build something. Now you tell me to leave."

"Just saying it'd be a lot safer. This is Ollie's turf."

"Won't his own gang be after him, though? Don't they hate snitches?"

"Probably," McClaren said. "But the guy he turned in wasn't connected to them. I don't know, maybe Ollie can make the case for what he did just so he could get out and get back at you."

"Good to know everybody's okay with this, as long as it's just me getting killed."

CHAPTER 2

I was in deep shit and needed help, so I'd called my friend J.C. Reed, who was always full of good advice, even if I seldom took it. He'd agreed to meet me for breakfast, and I was waiting in the diner with a headache and a mug of coffee, wishing it was a tumbler full of whiskey.

After McClaren's news the night before, sleep had been impossible. The ghosts and shadows of my past had come to haunt me. They always appeared when things got bad, and the current situation was ripe for a dead-person reunion inside my head. My fitful night had left me frayed around the edges, more so since it was a beautiful spring morning in Portland, and everyone seemed relentlessly cheerful and happy, as if in counterpoint to my misery.

J.C. came in to the diner, but kept stopping to talk to people he knew. As a journalist for *The Maine Times*, he met a lot of folks, and had friends everywhere. Plus, he bore an uncanny resemblance to Ernest Hemingway, white hair and beard trimmed just so. He always made fun of the comparison, but I knew he was flattered by it. I glowered at him, wishing he'd quit glad-handing and get his ass over to me.

He finally plopped into the bench seat across from me in the booth, beaming.

I gave him a sour look. "You running for mayor?"

"Jealous that I have friends?"

"Nice of you to finally make it, through your throngs of admirers."

"The price of fame," he said, airily waving his hand, playing it to the hilt.

"Glad someone's in a good mood."

"Are we Mr. Cranky-Pants this morning? On a glorious day like this? You look like hell, by the way."

My response was to toss him the letter I'd received in the mail the afternoon before. He looked at me, then pulled a small pair of reading glasses from the breast pocket of his shirt and put them on. He peered at the sheet of paper, holding it at arm's length until his eyes adjusted.

"Eviction notice?" He read some more. "Oh. On the building where your martial arts studio is, that whaddya call it?"

"Dojo," I replied. "Yeah. Months of renovations and thousands of dollars to get it looking nice, and now it's all flushed down the tubes."

"Looks like you've got to be out in thirty days."

"Right about the time I was going to have a grand opening."

J.C. shrugged. "So you'll find another place, and be punching and kicking people before you know it."

"I've invested my sweat and money in this place. Most of what I had went to the renovations."

J.C. cocked his head. "Including your little windfall from our adventure last autumn?"

"Yeah, between that and the fees to your red-haired attorney friend."

"I told you he wasn't cheap," J.C. said, putting his glasses away.

"I hope he likes the new Mercedes. Or was it a sailboat?"

"Kept you out of jail, though, so I'd say he was worth it."

The waitress came by, set a mug in front of J.C., and without asking, poured it full from the coffeepot she held.

"Thank you, Emma," J.C. said, though she wasn't wearing a name tag. "I'll have the usual."

Emma looked at me.

"Eggs over easy with whole wheat toast and home fries, please." She nodded and stepped away.

"Doesn't talk much," I said.

"Downeast Yankee," J.C. said. "Doesn't talk any more than she has to." He passed the notice back to me. "What are you going to do?"

"Can I fight it?"

J.C. shrugged. "You can spend a lot of money hiring yourself a lawyer, but they own the building, and can pretty much do what they want. What grounds would you use?"

"It's not fair."

J.C. made a sound in his throat. "That is a very weak argument when it comes to business ... or law."

"I've been pouring my heart and soul into that place. That's all that's kept me going since Allison dumped me."

"I know, but that doesn't matter." He sipped his coffee. "No break in the ice with her?"

"She still won't talk to me. First I move in, then move back out so her cousin and kid have room, then she tosses me out for good for saving her cousin from jail."

J.C. toyed with a spoon. "Wasn't it because she would have preferred to see a little less of you on a professional basis?"

Allison was a nurse, and it was true that my investigations had resulted in too-frequent hospital care. But I didn't want to hear anything like the hard truth right now. I wanted someone to tell me things would get better. Even if they were lying.

"So you're taking her side?"

"Someone's a bit touchy. Feeling sorry for ourself, are we?"

"You're damn right," I said. "Because that's not even the worst of it."

"There's more?" J.C. raised his eyebrows. "Good Lord, why am I sitting near you? You'll probably have a meteor fall on your head any minute now."

"It's not funny," I said.

"Sorry, just wondering how it could get any worse."

I took a deep breath. "Ollie Southern's out."

J.C. stared at me. "How?"

"Damn feds cut him loose, because he ratted out somebody bigger."

J.C. sat back. "Oh, my."

"Yeah. So now I have to look over my shoulder every damned minute."

"How'd you find out?"

"McClaren was at my door last night."

J.C. nodded. "He's a good man."

"For a cop."

"He didn't have to tell you."

"Yeah, I know. He wasn't too happy about Southern being turned loose, either."

J.C. looked thoughtful. "I can look into it," he said. "Maybe even do a spotlight piece about how the government is releasing killers. Put some pressure on them."

"Sure," I said. "And when I turn up dead, nail those bastards to the wall for me."

I fell quiet, feeling my chest tighten from the mounting pressure of everything closing in on me. I balled up the napkin in my hand.

Emma returned, and gave us our plates, without a word. J.C. dug into his breakfast, but suddenly I wasn't hungry anymore. I was too busy watching the door, wondering if Ollie was stalking me even now.

CHAPTER 3

My soon-to-be-closed dojo was housed in a strip mall, and as I approached, I knew that something was out of place up ahead. It's a feeling you develop if you're in certain professions, ones that rely on your ability to anticipate a dangerous situation. My years of being a bodyguard and bouncer had developed my sense for things that might mean trouble.

I needed to know if there was someone behind me, in case the black Lincoln SUV and the two guys waiting by it were just a distraction. So I stopped and bought a *Portland Press Herald* from a newspaper vending machine, and was able to scan in all directions. Not very subtle, in fact a dead giveaway, but I could see nothing suspicious behind me.

Ahead of me, though, were two very out-of-place men. They didn't hold themselves like cops or Feds, and were too well-dressed to be either. The suits were excellent, made of expensive material, and cut well. I'd seen a lot of mobbed-up guys in places like Vegas and Miami that dressed like this. Someone from my past life?

One guy looked to be in his late-thirties, and the other had a few years on him. The younger one had short, black, spiky hair and designer stubble, that carefully groomed, two-day-old growth of facial hair. The look was supposed to be cool and hip. The older guy sported a graying ponytail and a neatly trimmed beard.

The clothes indicated too much money, the kind that always meant trouble. They could be hoods, especially with the shiny expensive ride, but they didn't project physical menace. Their body language was all wrong; they were too much at ease, not expecting any danger. One had a takeout cup of coffee in his hand. I looked closely, but couldn't detect the telltale bulge of a gun beneath either of the tailored suits. No ankle holsters, either.

Lawyers, maybe? Was this about the eviction? In any case, I was sure I wouldn't like whatever they had to tell me. Might as well get it over with, but I decided to have a little sport.

I managed to get right up behind them before I spoke. "Can I help you gentlemen?"

Ponytail jumped, and spilled some of his coffee. The other guy's mouth fell open, as he looked around to see where I'd come from. They recovered, gave a little chuckle to show there were no hard feelings, and introduced themselves.

"Thornton White," said Ponytail, shaking the coffee off.

"Jens Macon," said Spiky-hair, sticking out his hand. I didn't want to shake it, but I did anyway.

"And you're Zack Taylor," said the older one.

"Yup. What can I do for you?"

They exchanged smiles and a knowing look. "This is your lucky day."

My laugh sounded bitter, even to me. "I sincerely doubt that."

"Can we come in?"

I unlocked the front door of the dojo and held it open. They stepped inside, and I turned on the lights. They looked around, nodding. I couldn't fathom why they were here. Maybe they'd heard about the eviction, and were scouting the place for something.

"So what's the deal?"

Ponytail finished his coffee, found a trash can in the corner to toss it into, and rubbed his hands. He looked at his partner, then puffed up before he spoke, like he was presenting an award. "How'd you like to be in movies?"

"What?"

"Movies. We represent K-Star Films, and want you to consultant on our latest action hit."

"You've got to be kidding." I looked from one to the other. No, they were serious. "Looks like you wasted a flight from L.A."

"We're shooting local, right now," Ponytail said.

I smiled. "An action film in Maine?"

Ponytail nodded, making a face. "Yeah, I know. But the money man lives out here. Doesn't like to travel, so he wanted it done where he could keep an eye on things."

"We heard about you," Spiky-hair said. "Someone who saw your fight last summer was very impressed. He says you know what you're doing, and you'd be a good addition to the film."

Ponytail chimed in. "We want you to make it real."

I started laughing. In spite of all the crap going on, it was refreshing. "That's what all this is about?"

They nodded vigorously, smiling all the while.

I shook my head. Most of the movie biz people I'd met were almost as bad as the mob guys I'd been around. I had too much on my plate right now to deal with their special kind of crazy. "Thanks, guys, but not interested."

Their smiles faltered, and they stared at me like I'd just turned down an offer of immortality. Maybe that's what they thought they were offering.

"You're joking, right?" Ponytail's voice had an edge, like I'd insulted him.

"No."

Spiky-hair almost whined. "But everyone wants to be in a movie."

"Not me. Sorry, fellas."

Their brows were furrowed as they exchanged looks again. "What would change your mind?" Ponytail shifted into intense salesman mode. "What do we need to do to make this deal happen?"

I shrugged. "Just not my thing."

Spiky-hair took a half-step closer. "Do you know who's directing? Bruce Taggart."

He showed such reverent awe that I laughed. "So?"

"So?" Ponytail looked like he'd been slapped. "He's just the best fucking action film director there is today. He made *Striking Dragon* with Jackie Chan, fer chrissake!"

"Well why not get him, then?"

"Who?"

"Jackie Chan."

Ponytail shook his head. "He's under contract for two more films. We can't touch him for 18 months."

"Bummer." How much more could I mock them before they got mad?

"Fuckin' A. But we got a great script."

I snapped my fingers. "You want a consultant, go ask Danny Thibodeaux, the Champion of Portland. He's dying to be in a flick."

They exchanged another look. I wondered what they'd do if they didn't have each other for confirmation.

Ponytail grimaced. "We can't use him."

"Why not? He's good at what he does. And he wants it, unlike me."

They looked embarrassed now. Spiky-hair spoke. "We, uh, did give him a try."

"What happened?"

Ponytail waved his hand. "He only wants to act. Came to the meeting, demanded we give him a screen test. So we did. But the guy's stiff as a fucking board. He can't act, plain and simple."

"That bad?"

"Yeah, every jamook thinks they're going to be the next Mel Gibson. You know, they see it done, and it looks easy.

But up in front of that camera, it's different. Acting natural, like you're not acting, is the hardest thing. And he can't do it. But he wouldn't let it go. We would have stuck him in a walk-on or in the background somewhere, but he kept being an asshole. We get enough of that shit."

"Did you tell him this?"

"Well, we tried to be nice, but the goddamned clown wouldn't listen. Ever try to say 'fuck off' to a coked-up karate fighter?"

Spiky-hair shot his partner a look like he'd spilled the beans, and Ponytail frowned.

Spiky-hair jumped in. "So we did the old 'we'll call you,' which everyone but this dipshit knows means 'get lost'."

I nodded, as I realized something. "He came to see me awhile back, telling me about this big fight, and trying to get me into it."

"Oh, Christ. He was desperate to get us to commit to something. So he pitched us on this exhibition thing. Said if we see him in action, we'd get all excited, that kind of shit. So we say 'yeah, whatever' just to get rid of him."

"And then he came around bugging me."

"Sorry, man. But look, we need you. Al was at your fight. He's got a good eye, and he said you're the real deal."

"Well, I don't know what to tell you."

"Tell us yes." This was from Spiky-hair. I was beginning to fear whiplash from the constant volleying of the conversation between them. "This could be a very lucrative deal."

Ponytail tucked a card into my shirt pocket. "Here's my number. You think it over. This could be your ticket to the big time."

"Funny, that's just what Thibodeaux said."

Dale T. Phillips

CHAPTER 4

The movie guys finally left, but under such protest that I almost had to get physical. If you think aggressive insurance salesmen are tough to get rid of, try some over-privileged Hollywood suits. They just couldn't come to grips with the fact I didn't want their ticket to fame and fortune.

The only recent occasion on which I'd gone to the movies was to take Allison on a date, and that hadn't ended well. Thinking about it was another reminder of how badly I'd messed up. She just couldn't put up with the violence in my life. When she'd broken up with me, I'd poured myself into the task of upgrading this place, channeling my energy, and giving myself a purpose, to keep from coming completely unglued.

The studio was quite an improvement from the dump I'd taken over, and I didn't relish the thought that all my time, effort, and money might have been for nothing. I felt hollow inside, and the beginnings of panic. After a lifetime of rootlessness and running away from things, I'd finally found reasons to stay in one place and make a real life, but one by one they were slipping away from me.

Sitting still and worrying about it wasn't going to solve anything. For me, action was always preferable. I looked at the copy of the *Portland Press Herald* I'd bought, and took out the real estate section. I sat in my office and studied the listings for commercial properties to lease. There were half a dozen possibilities that met my specifications.

The money was a definite worry, sure, but right now I had to have something to do, or I'd start feeling even sorrier for myself, and go deeper into my downward spiral.

I took a drive to check each location, to see if it would be a good spot to open a studio. Two looked really good, two were okay, one would work only as a last resort, and one would never do.

Back at my office, I called the number for the first property, explained who I was and that I was interested in the place for a potential martial arts studio.

The guy on the other end hemmed and hawed, and said he couldn't rent to me, that there was too much potential for a lawsuit. I explained that I carried insurance against such an occurrence, but he wasn't interested. He hung up, and I silently cursed our litigious society.

On to number two. I got a woman on the other end this time, repeated my spiel about renting, and got the same response. At least she listened five minutes longer, but the end result was the same. She would not rent the place for a dojo. The tenants next door wouldn't like it.

After that call, I tried to rationalize that maybe the best locations were hedging their bets against a certain type of business. So if I moved down the ladder, someone had to be hungry enough to lease me a property.

However, the third and fourth places I called gave the same response. In desperation, I called the last potential place on my list, and the guy first asked me to repeat my name, and then asked me to hold. He finally came back and said he couldn't rent to me. I hung up and stared at the phone. What in hell was going on?

The anger rose in me like a tide coming in. Someone was messing with me, and I wanted to find out who.

I called the number for the very last place, the one I'd ruled out. They told me that the guy who was renting it was currently on a job down on Marginal Way, and I got directions.

The spot was a building site, with a warehouse on the other side. The guy I wanted was in a construction trailer, standing over a set of blueprints on his desk.

"Bob Levine," he said, extending his hand.

"Tom Finn," I replied. I wanted the conversation to go beyond my name, and if 'Zack Taylor' was one of the flags for these refusals, I didn't mind lying.

"So, Tom," Bob said. "What kind of business you want to open up there?"

"My sister was thinking of opening a dance studio."

Levine's eyebrows went up so far they almost met his hairline. "Dance studio? In that neighborhood?"

"I admit it wasn't my first choice. But it's close to home for her, so she's interested."

"I see," he said. "Lease is a minimum one-year, here's the rate." He handed me a sheet of paper.

"I'll have to talk it over with her. We're thinking of sharing it with another business, make it easier to pay the lease."

"Good idea. What other business?"

"Some guy my sister knows. Wants to run karate classes or something." I watched his face.

The guy stiffened, his gaze shifting to the side. "Ah, we might have a problem."

"How so?"

"We don't lease to any karate guys. Had a big problem with that before. Major lawsuit."

"Did you now?"

"Yeah, real mess," the guy said. "So it's like, policy, you know."

I leaned forward. "That's very interesting Bob, as every owner in the area with a similar property has that same policy."

"How's that?"

"You'd turn down a big chunk of change for a lease on a crappy unit in a bad spot. That says you're lying, Bob."

"Now hold on just a goddamned minute—"

I reached over and grabbed two fistfuls of his shirt. "Who the hell told you not to lease? Who was it?"

The door to the trailer opened, and a guy in a hardhat stuck his head in. "Mr. Levine, we got a—"

I turned my head, and Levine socked me one in the jaw. He was a beefy guy, and it was enough to make me release my grip on his shirt. He took a step back and put his hands up in a boxing stance. "You want some more?"

I did. I really wanted someone to pound on right now, take out my frustration. But I suddenly realized this wasn't the time or place, and that Levine wasn't even the real enemy.

"How about I leave with no hard feelings if you tell me who gave you the word?"

Levine barked out a laugh. "Figure it out yourself, asshole. You're the guy, aintcha? Yeah. Well you got some bad enemies in this town."

No shit, buddy. If you only knew.

CHAPTER 5

Back at my dojo, the security monitor on my desk showed a trio of strangers approaching the front door. In the past, I'd had some trouble with unwanted visitors to the studio, so I'd installed closed-circuit cameras at the front and back, to give me a heads-up on who was coming.

Two men and a woman. The lead guy who held the door for the others was young and small, but dapper-looking in a pricey, modern-cut suit. The other man looked rather like a globe, tipping the scales at a good three-fifty, at least. He had a scarf, or rather an ascot, around his thick neck, and a butter-yellow sport-coat over a garish, multi-colored shirt with a huge floppy collar.

The woman wore expensive designer clothes that were made to look casual, but they really helped her figure, which didn't need any help at all. She wore a scarf to cover her hair, and overlarge sunglasses. I could see a fair amount of jewelry, and she carried a handbag that looked like you could stuff a couple of small dogs into it, with room left over. I hoped she didn't have a purse dog, as I had trouble keeping a straight face for people like that. A mob boss's wife got pissed at me once, when I laughed at the way she baby-talked to her ball of purse fluff.

I went out to see what fresh hell this would be. The small guy came forward to greet me, all young, crisp-looking and efficient.

"Raymond Billings," he said, sticking out a hand. "And you must be Zack Taylor."

"If I must," I said. "What can I do for you?"

"This is your lucky day," Billings said.

I resisted the urge to kick his shins. "People keep saying that to me, and it's still not true."

Billings' smile faltered for a moment, and then returned. "Well it is, because Miss Cerise would like to meet you." He nodded his head to indicate the woman behind him.

"Well, why doesn't she come over, then?"

Billings looked pained. "Janelle Cerise is a superstar."

"Of what?"

"You're kidding, right?" His eyes widened when I shook my head. "She was in the biggest film of last summer, and her last three movies have grossed over a billion."

I shrugged. "I don't watch many new movies. I like the older ones, though, with Bogie, Hepburn, Gregory Peck, that kind of thing."

Billings swallowed hard. He leaned in, earnest and hushed. "You're putting me in kind of a bind, here, Zack."

I thought he was being a little forward by putting us on a first-name basis so quickly, but I wasn't going to get offended just yet.

Billings went on. "Miss Cerise is accustomed to being treated like the superstar she is. She's taken quite a risk of being recognized and hounded by the press, just to come here to talk to you. Could you at least walk over and tell her what a big fan you are?"

I stepped past Billings and gave a slight nod of greeting as I approached. "Miss Cerise. I understand you're in movies."

She looked me up and down and laughed, a delightful musical trill that made you want to hear more.

"Isn't he funny, Bernard?" The woman said to her companion. "How nice to meet you, Mr. Taylor." She looked to be in her late twenties. Her voice was soft and warm and full of promise, and her perfume was subtle but enticing.

She extended a hand as if she was a queen bestowing a favor upon a peasant. I considered for a brief moment whether to be a real jerk and give the hand a good country shake, but decided instead to play the part. I took her proffered hand and pressed my lips to it, while I looked into her eyes. She arched a brow and removed her sunglasses. Her eyes were a beautiful violet, with full lashes and enough power to drop most men in their tracks. I was certainly not immune to her charms, which were considerable.

"This is Bernard," she said, indicating the rotund man next to her. "Say hello, Bernard."

"How do you do," said the man, with a British accent that sounded fake. I shook his hand, but it was moist and soft, and I had to resist the urge to wipe my hand on my pants.

"Zack," she said, putting a hand on my arm. "I want you to come work with me." She looked me right in the eyes. She knew what effect she had on men. I was supposed to melt, and damn near did. I hadn't been with anybody since my breakup with Allison, and this woman would have tempted St. Anthony.

I swallowed and managed to get out some words. "Thank you for the honor, but I'm afraid I'm not available at this time."

The lovely eyes narrowed, and I took a bit of perverse pleasure in my response. She wasn't used to being refused. She recovered quickly, however, and threw out another few thousand watts of smile.

"Well, I am quite disappointed, Zack. I was so looking forward to it. I would consider it a personal favor if you would change your mind. You know where we'll be when you do."

I didn't actually, but said nothing. Billings shot me a look of anguished disbelief. Janelle Cerise turned and left, followed by Bernard, followed by Billings, in a parade.

The lingering scent of Janelle Cerise's perfume clashed with the pungent odor of Bernard's cologne. I knew I'd be thinking about her for a while, and what a fool I was for turning her down.

Things were getting more bizarre by the minute. What else was coming my way?

CHAPTER 6

I needed to see J.C. again. I was being desperately needy, and likely annoying as hell, but my head was spinning from all that was happening. Some people in trouble turn to drink, others to drugs, or something else. I turned to a reliable friend.

J.C. was in his downtown office, typing away furiously. Seeing that he was hard at work, I took a seat in the corner and picked up one of the past issues of the *Maine Times*.

After about ten minutes, J.C. stopped to read over what he'd done, clicked a few final keys with a triumphant flourish, and looked up at me. "My company at breakfast wasn't enough for you?"

"Things have gone even farther into left field since then," I said. "I need to talk to you again. Can I buy you a drink?"

We took a short walk to a nearby watering hole that J.C. liked, with muted lighting, worn, dark wood, and private spaces. There was no blaring music, unlike a lot of bars, so you could actually talk to each other and hear what was said.

We took a table in the back. It was early, so there wasn't a server on, and the bartender came over to get our drink order.

"Mr. Reed," he said. "Always a pleasure."

"Same here, Jimmy. How'd the Sox finish up this afternoon? They were ahead 6-4 in the seventh."

Jimmy made a face. "They blew it, 7-6, giving up three in the last inning."

J.C. shook his head. "Damn shame."

"Straight up. They need a better closer."

"Well, I'll drown my sorrows with three fingers of the good stuff, since my compadre here is paying."

Jimmy nodded and looked at me. I ordered a club soda with a lime. Jimmy went to get our drinks, and J.C. smiled at me. "Your money is well spent. I found you some help. Freddy Barmakian is a good property attorney. He can look into your lease agreement, see if there's any wiggle room."

"Great," I said. "Because there's something fishy going on with that. You won't believe what happened when I tried to find a new place today." I recounted the story.

J.C. frowned. "That's odd."

Jimmy glided back and set down a thick-bottomed glass in front of J.C. and a tall tumbler for me. He slipped away without a word. J.C. held up his glass for a moment, turning it slightly to catch the contents in the light. He tipped the glass to me and took a sip with his eyes closed. A smile spread across his face.

"And what Scottish glen is that from?" I said. His answer sounded like a strangled gulp.

I sipped my club soda. "Strange as that rental business was, even weirder were my visitors. First, two suits from a movie studio made me an offer to be a consultant, whatever the hell that means."

"Whatever else it means, it will likely supply the funds to pay Freddy. Did you talk money?"

"No. I, uh, turned them down."

J.C. smacked his forehead with a palm. "Of course you did. Should I ask?"

I toyed with my drink, my thoughts slipping back to my past. "A lot of movie people hung out with the hoods I used to work for, and the two groups had a lot of similarities.

Arrogant, sleazy, with way too much money, and no class behind it. They like to run over people, and use their money and power to get away with all kinds of behavior that would land anyone else in jail. They've got no regard for anyone not part of their circle, with an exaggerated sense of self-importance and entitlement."

J.C. sipped some more of his drink. "For a guy who kicks people as much as you do, you speak well at times."

"Thank you. I really didn't like the movie people I saw. You can only hang out with them if you're shallow like they are, or you shut yourself off emotionally. And I did. It cost me, though. I'm trying not to be like that anymore."

"Fair enough. But I take it your war chest isn't deep enough to pay Freddy in the event of a protracted legal battle."

"Not even close."

"So maybe you should consider their offer."

I sighed. "Seems they really want me, too, for some reason. They sent Janelle Cerise to ask me personally."

J.C. almost spit out his Scotch and looked like he was peering at me over his reading glasses, which he didn't have on. "Janelle Cerise. Are you telling me *the* Janelle Cerise was in your place today?"

"Yeah, why?"

"Because she's a big movie star, dummy. They don't normally come out to the unwashed masses like that."

"Well, she did, with some companions."

J.C. leaned forward. "So what's she like?"

I smiled. "You've got a crush on a movie star?"

"You would, too, if you'd seen her in the skin-tight catsuit she was wearing in her last film."

"Maybe I should start going to the movies."

"So how does she look in person?"

"Quite fetching, I have to admit."

"Did you just say *fetching* about Janelle Cerise? Dear Lord." J.C. sat back, looking pained.

"Okay, I'll admit it. She's a smoking hottie. Smells good, too. Very nice perfume."

"What did she say to you, troglodyte that you are?"

"She wanted me to come work with her. She said she'd consider it a personal favor."

J.C. gritted his teeth. "And you said no, you simple idiot. I may have to kill you myself, on general principle."

"Anyway, she didn't seem happy I turned her down, after a personal appeal and all. Probably not used to people saying that."

"You think?" J.C. looked thoughtful. "On the other hand, they may just assume you're playing hard to get to drive up the price. Something they do a lot. The more you resist, the more they'll want you. So they'll be back."

"Who will they send this time? Twelve dancing girls?"

"If you turned down Janelle Cerise, they'll probably think you're gay."

I played with the straw in my drink. "I could certainly use the money. But I don't know anything about the movies."

"Quit whining, and let them worry about that. You just smile and do what they tell you, and take the money. Besides, have you got anything better to do right now? With your studio being taken away, you'll just sit around going crazy. This will keep you occupied, so you don't do anything stupid."

I looked at him, and he nodded at me. "Yes, you know I'm right."

"I guess so," I said. "But all this stuff going on, and with Ollie out, I'm wondering if it's some karmic payback."

"You're still feeling guilty about those people that died up in Mill Springs, aren't you? That wasn't your fault. And you saved that girl."

"But—"

"But, your butt. It's just life. You're getting all the bad things at once, instead of spread out, like most other people. Shall I tell you something to cheer you up? A silver lining to your cloud?"

I smiled. "Please."

"There's another reason you should work on the movie, apart from the money."

"What's that?"

He smiled. "Legitimacy. If Allison sees you doing something that doesn't involve punching people and getting hurt, she might be more disposed towards your wooing of her."

"Wooing," I repeated. "Why do you talk like that?"

He swallowed more of his single-malt and smiled. "Because," he said, taking on a rolling Downeast accent, "I am one wicked smart fella."

I shook my head. "I hate to say it, but you are. That's why I asked you for advice."

J.C. set the glass down. "And you're actually taking good advice for once?" The accent was gone. "Maybe you are learning."

Dale T. Phillips

CHAPTER 7

My head hurt from all my thoughts about the current situation rolling around and colliding like a truckload of loose bowling balls. It was too much to handle. Everyone wanted something: Ollie wanted revenge, someone wanted to close my dojo, a bunch of strange people wanted me on their movie set, and worst of all, I wanted Allison, but she didn't want me anymore.

The shadow of Ollie Southern haunted me, making me brood about death. There were too many dead people in my history: those I'd loved, those I'd fought, and those I'd tried to save.

Being with J.C. at the bar hadn't been a good idea. The thought of liquor was a powerful craving, for I'd found long ago that enough alcohol could temporarily wash away my ghosts. Of course, it washed everything else away as well.

So I was back at the dojo, and not in the best of moods. I wanted to go back to my room and try to forget, maybe work out, or take a hot shower and hope for some sleep.

There was a knock at the front door, and I jumped a little. No one could see in because of the big paper sheets I'd put up for privacy, but I had a way of seeing who was out there. I hustled back to my office and looked at the security monitor.

A tall guy stood in the doorway. He had a good build, longish blond hair, and he was whistling. He bounced on the balls of his feet, but there was no menace in his demeanor. He knocked again. I considered. If he was from Ollie, he wouldn't have announced himself this way, so he was probably someone else from the movie studio.

I opened the door, and he all but bounded in, full of energy. He looked around, nodding as if in approval, and turned to me. He had to be another movie star, because his smile was so bright, I almost needed sunglasses.

"Can I help you?" I asked, but I had that sinking feeling.

"You're Zack Taylor."

"Yes."

"I'm Claude Conway."

He looked at me like he expected me to be impressed. So I raised my eyebrows in a silent question.

"Claude "The Claw" Conway?" he said, prompting me. When I didn't respond he continued. "The actor."

I shrugged. "Okay, so what do you want?"

"You're kidding, right? This is some kind of put-on."

"Look," I said, as he went to the heavy practice bag that hung in a corner. "I'm really not in the mood for—"

He screamed with a powerful yell and let fly with a series of kicks and punches to the bag, while I stood and watched. His technique was kind of sloppy, more show than power. He finished with an eagle claw pose, as if he was gripping a throat.

He looked at me, huffing for breath. "You telling me you didn't see *Teeth of the Dragon?*"

I shrugged. "Nope."

"*Tail of the Dragon? Fire in Autumn?*"

I shook my head.

"You don't watch movies?"

"Some," I said. "Haven't seen those, though."

"Really? You gotta get out more."

"Probably. What exactly did you come here for? To hire me for the movie?"

"I want you to teach me."

That caught me up. "What? Martial arts?"

"Yeah, I talked to the guys. They said you turned them down. Guess I should've figured you didn't know much about film. But you know martial arts, that's for sure. Come by and show me some stuff, and I can do it in the film."

I shook my head. "That's not really the way it works."

He smiled. "Can it work for five grand a week?"

I looked at him, thinking I could probably overcome my dislike, if I was overpaid to that degree. "You people are insane."

"You think we're crazy Hollywood types?"

"Something like that."

"I get that. I feel the same way sometimes. That's why I don't live in L-A. Too much of a scene there. I like it quieter. Got a little horse farm up near Fresno."

It caught me up short. More painful memories flooded in. Fresno was where I'd grown up, and where my brother had died. Had Conway known I was from there? "Fresno?" I said. "You're kidding. Nobody who works in L-A lives up that far up."

"You know it, huh? Raisins and turkey farms, right?"

"Yeah." At least he knew something about it.

"See, I've got my own little world there. When I finish a picture, I drive up there and kick back for a while. Get my head together, you know?"

"I have a hard time imagining that," I said.

"Only if you look on the surface of things," he replied, with a serious expression.

"Well," I said. "You came here because you want some techniques for a movie. That kind of thing is a shadow, not real. What we do here in the dojo is real. We do it with honor and respect for the martial arts we study. I don't see that with you folks."

"And you think we're all like that," he shook his head.

"Until I find out otherwise."

"I want a teacher who goes beyond," he said. "Who can show me the real meaning of what I'm doing, who can look through the surface to see the person underneath."

"Uh-huh."

"Hey, I've got a Black Belt. It's not just for the films, I think it makes me a better person. Helps me find my center."

I shrugged. "I don't take private students until they prove themselves in class with everyone else. If they show me they have a real spark within them, then maybe."

"You know I can't take a class with everyone else," he said. "It would be a mob scene. But do you know what it's like, being a star and having people thinking you aren't a real person? Believing you're just some shallow pretty-boy? Trying hard for years to get some respect? I'd like you to come and help me out. I'm asking you."

He sounded sincere, but I had my doubts. Maybe he really was a good actor.

Anyway, the money would be useful in saving my ass. And there was always the Allison angle. So I'd take the job, even though it felt like selling out.

"Okay, you talked me into it. Where do I go?"

"Great," he said. "The studio car will come pick you up in the morning. We start early, and do long days. Can you be ready at six?"

"As long as I don't have to be nice to anyone at that time."

He laughed, and put a hand on my shoulder, which I'd never cared for from strangers. "I like you, Zack. Thanks for saying yes. It'll be good working with you. See you on set."

He walked out, and I wondered just who had conned who.

CHAPTER 8

The next morning, I was showered and waiting at the dojo when the vehicle from the studio pulled up, a monstrous black SUV. I opened the rear door and got in, seeing my old buddies, White and Macon. Since I'd forgotten which was which, I'd continue to think of them as Spiky-hair and Ponytail.

"You folks start early," I said, yawning.

"Time is money," said Ponytail from the passenger side. He held an enormous takeout coffee cup, and I wondered if we'd someday be up to the size of buckets.

"So where are we headed?" I asked from the back. Spiky-hair shot his buddy a look from his spot at the steering wheel.

Ponytail cleared his throat. "We've got five locations all over town, but today we're on set at Fort Williams."

I felt like I'd been tasered. Fort Williams was a huge open park by the sea, out in Cape Elizabeth, a big tourist landmark that contained the world-famous Portland Head Lighthouse.

It was also where I'd killed a man the year before.

The man had murdered my friend Ben Sterling, and made it look like a suicide. He was part of a crime syndicate, and

I'd flushed them out and taken them on, and almost died myself.

Sons of bitches. That explained the look between them. They knew, they had to. It had been all over the news at the time, and they'd found out.

I licked my lips. "You guys aware I got into some bad shit out there?"

They tried not to react, but weren't successful. Ponytail sipped from his pail of coffee. "I might've heard something about that."

"What did you hear?"

"That you went up against some crime boss and his gang. Bunch of guys, lot of guns. And you came out alive."

I sat without saying anything, my insides churning. I ran it through my head. Things clicked into place. "That's the reason you guys wanted me."

They exchanged another look, and Ponytail spoke. "The financial backer of the film, a Mister Harada, or *The Money*, as we call him, is very old-school Japanese, big samurai fan. He lives on an island off the coast here. Our guy was at your fight with that Thibodeaux guy. He was real impressed, went back and told Harada about you, that you were a real kind of warrior. Harada had been trying to get his ducks in a row to get a big action film done up here, and he started paying attention to you."

Another shadow. I'd had no idea.

"And when the papers reported the whole thing, he followed the case. He's crazy about this warrior ethic shit. He finally got the package put together for the movie, and here we are."

I sat in silence. These people truly were insane. "What if I didn't want anything to do with it?"

Ponytail turned in his seat to smile at me. "You're here, aren't you?"

And so I was. But whether I stayed or not depended on just how much I'd been manipulated. Had this mysterious Mister Harada actually pulled strings to get me evicted, to maneuver me into this? I knew the upper-echelon Japanese business mind, and knew that would be within their scope. If it was true, it was a move worthy of a chess master, but I hated the thought of being someone's game piece. Especially if they'd worked to close my studio before it even had a chance, and even more so if it stirred up the ghosts of my past. I was going to have a talk with this Harada.

We came to the entrance road of the park, and even at this early hour, it was bedlam, with cars, and people, and police everywhere. The park was open to the public at sunrise, and there was a crowd trying to get in, to see the movie shoot.

We were waved through, and drove down the road. The police had cordoned off the left side of the park, leaving the right open, with the wide expanses of picnic spaces, and the world-famous lighthouse towering by the sea. Somebody had some serious juice with town officials to get the necessary permits, the parks department, and the police. This was a big event, even though it was spring, not yet tourist season.

We got down to the small parking lot, where I could see the tip of land with the ruined fort where I'd almost died. I was quiet, fighting against the memories.

When we got out, we could hear the crowd buzz from a hundred yards away, as people pointed cameras or fingers at us. Maybe they thought we were movie stars, or maybe they were just bored.

There were squads of police at the lot, and we were passed through once more. We walked down the shore road to the point. I saw massive movie lights on dollies, large background screens, and about a hundred people, half of them in constant motion. To an outsider like me, it seemed total chaos.

"Let's go meet Taggart," said Ponytail. "Although I gotta warn you, he's a total asshole."

"All directors are assholes," said Spiky-hair. It was the first time I'd heard him speak on this trip. Maybe he wasn't a morning person.

43

We came up to a semicircle of about two dozen people. They were watching a pair of men who stood with three other people fluttering around them, dabbing them with makeup, holding up what I assumed was a light meter, and another giving instructions in a quiet voice. I recognized one of the men as my actor buddy from the previous night, but he wasn't looking in my direction.

One guy near us was shouting orders. When he stopped for a moment and sank back into a director's chair, Ponytail made his move. He brought me forward and made introductions.

"Bruce, this is the guy."

Taggart looked at me. He didn't quite scowl, but his expression was none too friendly.

"Okay, you're here. I know I'm supposed to be welcoming and shit, but I've got scenes to shoot. So just hang out and try not to get in the fucking way, okay?" Before I could answer, he jumped out of the chair and moved off, yelling. "Hey, asshole! Yeah, you! Move that light."

"Nice to meet you, too," I said, to the empty chair.

"Told ya," Ponytail said in my ear.

CHAPTER 9

Someone yelled for quiet, and everybody froze in place. I was impressed by the discipline. A scruffy man in shorts and a plaid shirt held up an electronic clapper and announced the scene. The director, Taggart, was peering into a monitor, one arm raised, as everyone but the two actors watched him.

"Go!"

The two actors exploded into motion. The guy on the left threw a wide roundhouse punch at Claude, who blocked it with his left.

"Cut!"

There it was, another moment of movie magic.

"Hostage scene," called the guy with the clapper. People were in motion again. Claude walked toward us, to a canvasback chair with his name stenciled on the back. He saw me and came over, hand outstretched.

"Hey, glad you made it. You'll get to see me in action a little later."

My reply was cut off by a guy who stepped in and spoke loudly. "Claude, can I see you for a second?"

Claude walked off with the guy, and I looked around.

"So where's this Harada?" I asked Ponytail.

"Doesn't come on set," he replied. "He's strictly a behind-the-scenes kind of guy."

"He's putting up the money, but doesn't need to see what's being done with it?"

Ponytail smiled at me. "Kind of like sausage. You like it, but you don't want to see it being made."

"I get it. So what happens next?"

"Cerise has her action scene. And Claude has a big fight scene later."

"Can't wait," I said, yawning.

The noise level increased, and I saw Cerise coming on set with four people around her. She showed a lot of leg in an elegant evening gown with a couple of artful rips in it. Her hair was mussed, and she had some makeup streaks on her face that I guessed were supposed to make her look like she'd been roughed up. She looked far too glamorous to have been roughed up, though, and damn sexy.

The crew prepared the scene, and Cerise took her place while a hulking bald guy stood behind her. Claude stood about fifteen feet away.

"Quiet on set," came the cry. The guy with the clapper made his call, and we all waited.

In the stillness, I heard the faint drone of a distant plane.

"Got some noise," said a man wearing giant headphones, sitting at a control board. We stood in silence, and the plane sound tapered off.

"Okay."

"Everybody ready."

The big guy put his arm around Cerise's throat from behind. Taggart was watching his monitor. "Go!"

I leaned in and whispered to Ponytail. "Isn't he supposed to say 'Action!'?"

"Ssshhh," he said.

Cerise struggled against the big man's grip. He held a prop gun in the other hand, and pressed the barrel against her head. "One more step and she gets it."

"Shoot him," Cerise cried. "Shoot the son-of-a-bitch!"

"I'm putting the gun down," said Claude.

46

I thought it wasn't too smart a move for the character. The bad guy would shoot him anyway.

The big man spoke again. "I've waited a long time for this, McAllister. Now you're gonna get it."

Cerise pretended to bite the man's arm. He yelped and let go, and she drove an elbow back, and stomped down on his instep.

"Cut!"

We went back to standing around. I was okay with that for now, because I'd been a bouncer and bodyguard, both of which required a lot of standing around being ready in case something happened, and as long as they were paying me, I could hang outside on a nice day and take a bit of boredom.

A tough-looking Japanese man was headed straight for us. Ponytail spoke softly. "That's Kenishi, Harada's security guy. Real hardass."

The man stood before us, and looked me up and down. He didn't even bow or nod, a notable sign of disrespect in his culture. He seemed to find me lacking somehow.

He spoke to me in a clipped tone. "Mr. Harada wants you to come to the island to speak with him."

"Does he, now?" I wondered if my sarcasm would make a crack in that stern face. Nope.

"The boat will be here at two o'clock. Be ready."

I grimaced as if I was truly pained. "So sorry. I'm kind of busy at two. Maybe some other time." I smiled with a big idiot grin.

Kenishi's eyebrows scrunched together, as did the muscles around his mouth. This guy got angry even faster than me. "You see him when he tells you. Mr. Harada is very important man."

"And I'm just a stupid *gaijin*, right?" I stared him down. "You have lost face by being so rude to me. Go tell Mr. Harada to send someone who asks, not demands." I then insulted him with a basic phrase of my very bad Japanese.

Kenishi's fists clenched, though his face showed nothing but a slight flaring of the nostrils. Admirable control for a guy who wanted to punch my lights out right about now. Something flickered in his eyes.

He bowed deeply, then looked at me with his head down, his gaze somewhere around my chest. "Mr. Taylor, please forgive my rudeness. It was inexcusable. I would not have my employer's important business compromised, and so I humbly ask your pardon. Please join us at two o'clock for a short boat ride to speak with Mr. Harada."

He looked up to see if it had worked. I'd have let him off the hook if his eyes hadn't been glowing with hate. I'd make the meeting, but I wanted one last little needling. "I'll think about it," I said, and turned my back on him. I heard him walk away.

A few beats later, Ponytail whooshed out his breath. "Holy shit, what were you thinking? That guy looked like he was ready to rip your head off."

"I don't like being bossed around."

"I guess the fuck you don't. Might want to dial it down a bit, though. Play the game. Don't piss off the money."

"That's just the errand boy. What do you know about Harada, anyway?"

Ponytail shook his head. "He's putting up thirty million dollars to make this film. That's all I need to know."

Spiky-hair was talking on his phone. He tapped Ponytail to follow him, and they walked off. I hung around, getting more bored by the minute. Since the crew took so long to set up each shot, there were long stretches of nothing much, then a few seconds of shooting.

I did spot an attractive young blonde woman who checked things against her clipboard. She even smiled at me once. But for the most part, all that was going on was people in motion while they moved things around.

It was ticking on towards noon, and I finally paid attention when three guys arrived, dressed as ninjas. They took their places around Claude on the set. The scene began, and they attacked him, one at a time, of course. Claude took a few hits, but triumphed over two of them before squaring off against the third. He and the baddie threw a few lines of tough-guy dialogue at each other, which took another half-hour to get right, with a half-dozen takes. The remaining ninja said to Claude that he "was going to hurt you real bad," and the action was as bad as the grammar.

They began the climactic fight. Claude backed up the stone stairs, leaving himself open to crippling blows in a number of ways.

"Cut!"

I shook my head, and saw a guy glaring at me. It was the loudmouth from before.

They called for a lunch break, and Taggart walked off, arguing with some guy in a suit. Claude came back to his chair, drinking from a bottle and wiping his face with a towel passed to him by an assistant.

"Whaddya think?" Claude said to me.

I shrugged.

"No, really," he said. "I want your honest opinion."

"Well," I replied. "If those guys are supposed to be ninjas, they're the world's worst. They had over a dozen chances to take you out. And then you backed up the stairs, which would've got you killed."

The loud guy was there, hands on hips. "And who the fuck are you?"

I kept calm, not showing anything in my face. The guy stepped closer. He was taller than me, a little over six feet, and he looked to be in good shape.

"I asked you a question, dipshit," he said to me. People around got very quiet and still.

"He's the Black Belt Mr. Harada wanted," offered Claude.

"Is he now?" Loudmouth continued. "Well I've got three Black Belts, and twenty years' experience as a fight coordinator."

"He might be right about the scene, though," Claude went on. "Maybe we should rethink it, or change the action a little."

Loudmouth's voice went up a few more decibels. "There! Are you fucking happy? Over a grand a minute, and now we've got extra work because you shot your mouth off."

"Hey, he asked my opinion," I said.

"Keep your fucking opinion to yourself." He jabbed me in the chest with a finger.

"Don't do that," I said.

"Tough guy, huh? Think you can take me?"

"I don't want to take anybody or anything. Just get out of my face."

"This is my set," he replied. "And I want you gone." He jabbed again.

I snapped out, grabbing his wrist with one hand and his elbow with the other, as I twisted and squeezed. It had been too fast for him to react, and was an effective joint lock, and I bent him over to get him off balance. He had no way out of it, and was at my mercy, for as long as I held it.

He hissed through clenched teeth. "Somebody get Security."

"Good idea," I said. "When I let you go, I don't want you doing anything stupid."

"I'll fix your ass," he said. "You'll never set foot on this set again."

"Heavens," I said. "However will I get by?"

A huge black guy in a security guard uniform parted the crowd and looked at the tableau before him. He held his hands at his sides, and his face was serene. When he spoke, his voice was deep, but mellow, the cadence calm. "Sir, please let Mr. Davis go."

"As long as he doesn't attack me again, I'd be happy to."

"I'm here now. Let's just keep calm."

"Sure thing," I said, and let go.

Davis stood up, massaging his elbow. He addressed the guard. "I want you to throw this fucker off the set. Right now."

"I was invited here by Mr. Harada," I said. I jerked a thumb at Davis. "So unless this clown has more juice than the money man, you might want to clear it with your boss first."

The guard looked at each of us in turn. "Let's go see Mr. Taggart."

The crowd stepped back to let us all through. I kept an eye on Davis, in case he got stupid and wanted to get physical again.

We walked over to where more than a dozen trailers were camped, and the guard rapped on the door of one with a knuckle the size of a ham-bone. After a moment the door cracked open. "Yes?"

"Mr. Davis here has got a serious issue with an invited guest of Mr. Harada."

"Oh, Sweet Jesus," said the voice. "Bruce? You better handle this."

After a beat, the door opened wide. Taggart stood there and looked unhappy to see us.

Davis spoke up. "This asshole was pissing all over how we shot the scene. Claude started talking about reshooting. I told this clown to keep his mouth shut, and he jumped me."

Taggart looked at him. "You're the fucking fight coordinator. Why didn't you just kick his ass?"

"I was assaulted at work. This is a union matter. You gonna throw him off the set, or am I making the call?"

Taggart made a sound of disgust. "You really going to play that card?"

"If I have to."

Taggart stepped back and threw the door open wide. "Get your asses in here and let's get this settled."

Inside the trailer was surprisingly spacious, even with all of us there. The guy in the suit Taggart had been arguing with was seated on a sofa at the far end, smoking a joint. I glanced at the security guard, who wasn't saying anything. Taggart scooped up an amber-filled highball glass, took a long drink, and sat in an overstuffed chair. "Now what the fuck is this all about, anyway?"

Davis jumped in again. "This guy's telling Claude the scene is bullshit. You feel like reshooting until he's happy?"

"No, I do not," said Taggart, looking at me. "What the fuck is your problem, anyway?"

"Claude asked me what I thought. So I told him."

Taggart looked at the man on the couch. "You believe this shit?" He cocked a finger at me. "I thought I told you to keep the fuck out of the way."

I shrugged. "You people are kind of touchy."

Taggart slammed the empty glass down on a side table. "We've got a hundred-fourteen people on payroll, and every minute costs a bundle. So if the fucking star asks for your fucking opinion, you tell him it's the greatest scene since Citizen Fucking Kane. Now I cannot have you around here pissing off my help. Even Mr. Pain-in-the-Ass Davis here. I can't have him filing a complaint with the union. So you are out of here, as of right now." Taggart looked at Davis. "Happy?" Davis nodded.

"Good," said Taggart. "Then get back to work, and kiss Claude's ass until he agrees we're good to go."

Davis left.

The guy on the couch cleared his throat. "Bruce, Mr. Harada is not going to be happy with this situation."

"Neither am I. But I heard this guy and Kenishi already got into it, too. That's two problems in one morning, and I've had enough."

"Look," I said. "I wasn't trying to cause trouble. Things kind of blew up fast. But I was supposed to catch a boat out to see Mr. Harada at two, and if he wants me to, I'll leave after that."

Taggart picked up the empty glass and looked at it. "Theo? Can you keep this prick out of everyone's hair until it's time for his little boat ride?"

"Yes sir, Mr. Taggart," the big guard rumbled from behind me.

"Good. Get him out of here, someplace out of sight. Give him some goddamn lunch if you can do it without him pissing anyone else off."

The guard opened the door to the outside and looked at me. I looked back at Taggart. "Always a pleasure, Bruce," I said, and made my exit.

Dale T. Phillips

CHAPTER 10

Once again, I'd proven what an idiot I was. I'd decided to take the job, thinking about Allison and the money, and here I was getting fired just a few hours later. While other people focused on their goals, I just ran at trouble until I got my ass kicked.

At least the big guard hadn't tried to get tough, or intimidate me. The good ones don't have to. He seemed like the real deal, not some twelve-dollar-an-hour imitation tough guy.

Outside the trailer, he started walking, and I kept up with him. He spoke, his voice low, so only I could hear him. "Thanks for not making this a problem."

I grinned at him. "You're not the one I want to piss off. Theo, is it?"

He looked at me. "Thelonius M. Burbee."

"Ah," I said. "M for Monk, no doubt. So your parents were jazz buffs, huh?"

"Yeah."

"Could be worse," I said. "Zack Taylor. I got named for a U.S. President no one's heard of, unless they're a historian." We shook hands. "So why is it Theo?"

"'Cause nobody knows how to spell it. They think it's The-*o*-lonius." Theo eyed me. "So what do you do, other than make a pain in the ass out of yourself?"

"Tried to run a dojo, until recently. But I did security work, before. I was a bouncer and a bodyguard."

He smiled in a friendly way. "Little guy like you?"

I laughed.

"I did hear you were good," he admitted. "You handled Mr. Davis pretty easy."

"He's only six feet tall. You'd rip my arms off and beat me with them."

He laughed. "Nah. I'd just tackle you and try to hold on, let my weight do the job."

"That would work," I admitted. "But you might be a little sore tomorrow."

He smiled.

"Long as I didn't get your knee," I added. I'd noticed a bit of a limp earlier.

He nodded. "You don't miss much, do you?"

"I'd guess you were offensive tackle."

"You'd be right."

"That knee keep you out of the pros?"

He shook his head. "Hadn't got that far. Junior year, LSU. Sucker popped out, and that was all she wrote. Without me playing, the scholarship money dried up, so I didn't get to finish. Funny how when they don't need you anymore, the free ride stops being free."

"Ain't it the truth?" I agreed. "And now you keep the peace around here."

"Yeah, it's mostly dealing with these Hollywood pricks."

"You didn't come with them? They knew your name. Well, almost knew it."

"'Cause they think it's funny, name like Theo." He grimaced. "Won't come right out and say it to my face, but they do. They wouldn't fly someone like me out from L.A. Strictly local talent."

"Local, huh?" I scratched my head. "Pardon me for saying this, but how many black security guards does Portland have?"

"Just me," he smiled. "My size and color are usually enough to stop trouble. They see the movies, so sometimes I put on the act, go all Samuel Jackson on their ass. Scares the shit out of most people. Think I'm gonna bust a cap in 'em or something."

I laughed. "So what do we do for the next two hours?"

"We get something to eat. They've got box lunches under that tent over there. You like turkey, roast beef, tuna, or veggie?"

"Tuna, please. Can't get my own? You don't trust me even just standing in line for a sandwich? I'm hurt."

"Yeah, guy like you causes trouble just by being around. And these people are prickly. Everything is a turf fight, showing whose dick is bigger."

"Sounds like a ton of fun."

"It's a pain in the ass. All these dicks and asses, and I'm the one getting fucked. You go wait over by that tree, and I'll grab the lunches."

Theo was back in under ten minutes, carrying three white cardboard boxes and two bottled waters. We strolled over to a quiet spot, and took out our sandwiches. While we ate, we talked some more.

I nodded to the extra box. "Somebody joining us?"

Theo shrugged. "I get hungry."

"So what can you tell me about this Harada?"

"Old-school Japanese. Came up here and made a pile in fishing. Has a small fleet of boats, one all-Japanese crew, maybe even a plane or two. Bought an island out in the harbor. Kenishi is his eyes and ears on the set. And I heard you went and got all up in Kenishi's face. That took some balls."

"No friend of yours?"

"It's like he's even more prejudiced than everyone else. Guy looks at me like I'm something he'd scrape off his shoe."

"Don't take it personally," I said. "Some old-school Japanese are like that, hate everybody who's not born in their country."

He shook his head. "Watch out for that one. Even I wouldn't like taking him on."

"Too late. I'm glad it's you babysitting me instead of him. That would get real uncomfortable fast."

"How'd you get so popular, anyway?" Theo had finished his first sandwich, and was already working on the one from the extra box.

"Somebody saw a fight of mine last year, and I guess word got back to Harada. So they came recruiting. I said no a couple of times, but they were persistent bastards. Even sent out Janelle and Claude."

Theo whistled. "Yeah, they want you bad. Them's the big guns, and getting those two to do anything extra isn't easy."

"Wish I knew for sure why they really want me."

Theo had been unwrapping a cookie from one of the boxes. "You really don't know?"

"Well, my ride let slip that it's because of the trouble I had out here last year. Maybe this Harada wants what he thinks is a genuine tough guy on the set."

Theo cleared his throat and set down his cookie. "Shit. I thought you knew."

"This isn't sounding good," I said.

"Maybe I shouldn't say anything." He looked around, then at me. "This movie. It's about that day. Your story."

"*What?*"

"How you took on a bunch of killers with no gun and survived."

"I don't believe this. They're doing a movie based on something that happened to me, and didn't even ask?"

"Guess they expected to dazzle you with all the glamor, and by the time you figured it out, you'd be flattered."

"If it's my story, what was that hostage horseshit with Cherise? There was none of that. And what about the freaking ninjas? There weren't any goddamn ninjas."

Theo looked at me with an expression of pity. "Welcome to Hollywood."

I scrambled to my feet, hurling my water bottle against a rock. The bottle was plastic, so it simply bounced off, ruining my dramatic gesture. "Forget about waiting until two o'clock. I'm going to see Kenishi and have him call the island and get that boat here right now. I'm going to have a little heart-to-heart with the guy behind this."

Theo's mouth was set with a pitying line. "You gonna tell a guy with his own island he can't film a movie?"

"Well, yeah, if it's based on something I did. I can sue the bastard."

Theo's smile looked knowing and sad. "His lawyers are more expensive than yours."

That made me stop and think. I'd have to hire another damned lawyer. I remembered the stiff attorney fees to keep myself out of jail, and shuddered. Plus, I already had one attorney working for me. Where was I supposed to come up with the money for another expensive court battle?

"Well, shit, I can't just let this go on. I could threaten to sue him, maybe that would get him to reconsider."

"Good luck with that," Theo said and laughed. "My man, they get sued all the time. That's why they have those high-priced suits on retainer. You're gonna have to come up with something better."

I nodded. "You're right, damnit. And I'm guessing appealing to his better nature won't do much good."

"Man don't get his own island by doing what other people say."

"What about honor? I heard he was old school."

Theo shook his head. "Look around. This is one major investment. He'd probably say this is honoring you."

I looked at Theo. "You are one hell of an unusual security guard."

He smiled and shrugged. "You gonna make any kind of plan before you go see the man?"

I spread my hands. "I got nothing. Maybe I can think of something on the boat ride over."

"Charge right in, huh?"

"Like a bull in a china shop. That's my usual style."

He nodded, looking out over the ocean. "You really take out four armed guys without a gun?"

"Five. I was stupid to do it, but they killed my friend. I got lucky."

"Damn. So I guess you'll just do whatever you want."

"Like the guy with the island. Sounds like we'll talk the same language."

Theo shook his head. "Guess you will at that."

"Can we go see Kenishi now? Ask about that boat ride?"

"Why the hell not?"

We walked over to the row of trailers set up for the actors and "important" people. Kenishi's was smaller than that of the stars, a nondescript unit in a cluster.

Theo knocked on the door. There was no response. He knocked harder.

"I don't hear nothing. Guess he ain't there."

"Did you try the door?" I hated to say it, but had to check to be sure.

Theo looked at me, but reached out a hand and turned the knob. He seemed surprised when it moved, and he pulled the door open.

"Mr. Kenishi?"

I tried to peer around Theo to the interior, but his bulk blocked my view. He leaned in to look around and backed down the set of steps. I slipped in.

Harada lay on the floor. There was no blood, no wound I could see. I put my fingers on his neck to feel for a pulse.

He was stone cold dead. I looked at Theo. "Shit," was all he said.

"You got that right," I replied.

CHAPTER 11

The police again. Like McClaren at my door, it was bad news time. Because of my past, I hated talking to them, but when you find a body, there's no way out of it. I was telling my story for the third time when I looked up at the new cop who had just stepped into view.

Oh, crap.

"You again," Sgt. Lagasse said. "Of course. A dead body, no wonder I find you here." He turned to the other cop and jerked his head. "I got this one."

Lagasse looked at me, toothpick twirling in the corner of his mouth. While McClaren had feelings, Lagasse had had too much bitter time on the job, and took it out on suspects, and even witnesses. "What, no smartass remarks?"

"I had nothing to do with this. We just opened the door and found him, that's all."

"Well, not quite all, is it? Way I heard it, you and the deceased got into it this morning."

I clammed up. Maybe I needed to call my red-headed lawyer again. Damn.

"You gonna talk to me, or are you gonna obstruct this investigation?"

I ground my teeth. "He came to tell me to catch a boat ride out to see his boss at two. He was rude, and I was rude back."

"Yeah, I'll bet you were."

"That was it. That was the only time I saw him, until the trailer."

"And why were you at his trailer?"

"I wanted him to call for the boat early."

"Why's that?"

"I was anxious to see his boss."

Lagasse pulled the toothpick out of his mouth and studied it. "You know, I been doing this a long time. When someone tells me something while holding back, I know it. And I don't like it."

I sighed. "I found out this movie is about what happened here last year. With me."

Lagasse replaced the toothpick. "Yeah, I wondered if you knew. So when did you find out?"

"About two minutes before we went to see him. Hey, I was never alone here the whole time I was on set. Ask around."

"I already did," said Lagasse, looking pleased. "But actually, you were alone. When the guard went to get your lunch."

Goddamnit.

"Be real slick for you to slip off and do the deed on a short break, then have an excuse to go find the guy. So I got a body, I got you with a motive, and opportunity. Any reason I shouldn't arrest you right now?"

"How about because I didn't do anything?" My voice was still level, but wouldn't be for long, if he kept this up. "Or doesn't that even matter to you anymore?"

"Thought I recognized that whiny voice," someone said behind me. I turned to see Mason Carter, the sleazebag reporter, standing there with camera at the ready. He snapped one off at the look of annoyance on my face.

Oh, shit, could this get any worse?

"Two assholes for the price of one," said Lagasse. Apparently he didn't like the reporter any more than I did. A point in his favor. "What are you doing here, Carter?"

"Checking out the murder, just like you," Carter replied, grinning. "It is a murder, right, Sergeant?"

"We have a deceased individual," Lagasse deadpanned. "No apparent cause of death. We'll know more after the Medical Examiner's report. So don't go calling it a murder until we find out if it is one."

"Possible murder," said Carter. "Gotcha. But I thought you were about to arrest this clown."

"What's it to you?"

"News. I'm a reporter, remember?"

"You're about as much a reporter as he is an upstanding citizen."

"He still owes me for that camera of mine he busted." Carter looked at Lagasse. "In your police station."

"You file a report?"

"You're a funny man, Sergeant. Just like our friend here. How come he's so quiet? It's not like him."

I tried to glare him away. "Why don't you get lost?"

Carter grinned. "What's the matter? Still sore over those pictures?"

The son-of-a-bitch had invaded my hospital room while I was recovering and published the photos he'd shot. I was clenching my fists. "You're lucky the Sergeant is here."

"Or what, you'd beat me up? You hearing this, Sergeant?"

"I kinda like it. I'd sell tickets. I know we'd get a crowd from the station."

"I'm not feeling a lot of love from you two," Carter said.

"Time for you to go," Lagasse said.

"Alright, alright. But I'll be watching." Carter snapped a couple of photos as he walked backwards. Lagasse watched him go.

"Jesus, he's annoying," Lagasse said. "Even more than you."

"Thanks a lot," I said. "You know, I'd always thought it was you that called to tip him off when I was at the station that day."

Lagasse looked at me, then shook his head. "I know we don't like each other, but the day I call a piece of shit like that with a tip is the day I turn in my badge."

"Sorry, then," I said. "So what now?"

"Now we go to the station, until we get word on what happened to the deceased. Then we take it from there."

"Am I under arrest?"

"Not yet. But maybe I'll get lucky, and find out he was murdered."

CHAPTER 12

Lagasse took me back to the Portland police station and parked me in an interrogation room, where I sat for what seemed like hours. As I got more agitated, I wondered how I kept getting into these messes. I'd taken a job I really didn't want, tried to do the right thing, but was once more under the scrutiny of the police.

They wanted me to sit and stew, but I got tired of being a good little suspect. I went to the door and eased it open a crack.

McClaren was talking, but he was out of sight, around the corner. "You telling me the governor's office is riding this one, too? I'm getting supremely tired of this shit. You people better lay off, or you can shove this job, and I'll have a press conference as to why."

"Settle down. All we want is a quick verdict on cause of death, verify that there was no foul play. Keep things calm." It was a man's voice.

"So we've got the fastest goddamn autopsy in state's history, because someone's got pull."

"We just want the medical examiner and your office to give it top priority."

"Yeah, sure. Anything else? Want me to wax the governor's car? Pick up his laundry?"

There was a slight pause. "We appreciate your cooperation, Lieutenant."

"Eat shit and die. You come down here sticking your nose in our investigations, and when we catch the sonsabitches, you turn them loose."

"You know Ollie Southern wasn't our fault. We had pressure from the Feds. We had to release him."

"Yeah, you must have put up one hell of a fight."

I exploded from the doorway, and turned the corner to see McClaren with a man in a brown suit. I grabbed the guy by the lapels and slammed him against the wall as I screamed in his face. "You little shit! Southern's coming after me because of you. You let a murderer go."

An arm locked around my throat, and hands seized parts of me and peeled me off the guy. I choked, and was flung back into the interrogation room, with three uniformed cops between me and the door. They had their batons out, and looked like they wanted to use them, but I was so mad I was ready to take them on anyway.

McClaren came in and pointed at me, shouting. "Sit down, goddamnit, or I'll put you in full restraints and throw you in a cell."

I coughed, getting my breath back, and realized I'd better do as he said. I groped for the chair and sat down.

He turned to the uniforms. "I got this. You guys did good. Go make sure our visitor is taken care of."

One of the uniforms gave me the hard stare as he went. I let it pass. My fury was already leaving me.

McClaren turned to me. "Don't ever attack anybody in my station again."

I rubbed my throat. "Your boys were pretty fast. Pretty rough, too."

"Goddamn good thing. I thought you were going to kill him. He's just the messenger, you know."

"I wanted to send him a message."

"Yeah, well, I think he got it. He actually pissed himself."

I snorted, and my anger dissipated completely. McClaren hid a brief smile behind a cough. "I told him you were here to ask for protection, because they'd released the man who was going to try to kill you."

"Very nice," I said. "Make them think twice, and bounce the blame for the crazy man right back to them and what they did."

"It'll still be another shitstorm."

"What in hell is going on, Lieutenant? Why is your office suddenly getting all this pressure?"

"That's not your concern."

"It is when they let killers go, who then come after me. Who's got that kind of juice, to be able to turn the screws on you guys so fast?"

McClaren shrugged. "People with power and money. Same old, same old."

"Would a guy named Harada have something to do with it? Guy making the movie?"

"Why you asking?"

"Because I found out the movie's about what happened to me out there."

McClaren frowned as he took this in. "I didn't know that."

"Yeah, imagine how pleased I was to find out. They hired me as a consultant, and didn't tell me what it was about. I was played, big time, so I want to know more about this guy. What the hell is a Japanese guy doing buying an island out in Casco Bay and doing a movie? Sounds a little eccentric, to say the least."

"I hear he's into fishing. Got an all-Japanese crew working a boat."

"Any of the locals get upset he hires his homeboys, instead of them?"

McClaren gave a thin-lipped smile. "Why is it we bring you in here for questioning, and you start pumping us for what we know?"

"Oh, come on. You know I didn't kill Kenishi."

"Actually, I don't know that. My gut tells me no, but we have to cross every *t* and dot every *i* on this one. High profile, as you heard. And I keep asking myself the same question."

"What's that?"

"Why is it dead people turn up whenever you're around?"

"All I did—"

"Save it," McClaren snapped. "Been there, done that, heard all the excuses. But once again, you were present when someone was found dead. What the hell were you doing out there, anyway? Crowd like that, Ollie Southern could have easily been watching you, waiting for a chance."

"I'm not going to live my life trying to figure out when Ollie may or may not show up."

"Your funeral," said McClaren.

"Look, they offered me a job. They were pretty insistent."

"They're insistent, but they fire you a few hours into it?"

I shrugged. "You know how it is."

McClaren laughed. "No, I don't. I know how it works for most people, but you arrive on a scene, and everything goes to shit."

"Thanks a lot." I clenched my fists under the table.

"Just calling it like it is."

"So can I go?"

"Not until we get a cause of death. Shouldn't be too long. We can't keep important people waiting."

I knew he wasn't talking about me. I rubbed my face with my hands. "I just want to get back to my dojo. While I still have one."

"Trouble?"

"They're kicking me out. I got an eviction notice, just before you came to tell me about Ollie. Now this."

McClaren actually looked sympathetic. "Tough break."

"You got that right. Can I at least go to the bathroom?"

"Long as you don't cause any trouble."

McClaren led the way out, and went off, and I found my way to the restroom. When I came out, the uniformed cop that had given me the hairy eyeball in the interrogation room saw me, did a doubletake, and walked on over.

I put up my hands. "Your Lieutenant didn't want any more problems."

"That's too bad," the cop said. "You looked like you wanted some action earlier."

"Yeah, I did, and there were three of you."

"Only one of me now," said the cop, spreading his hands. "Want to take a shot?"

"With your buddies here to put another chokehold on me? No thanks. How about you come down to my dojo sometime, off the clock, put your badge and gun aside, and you and me can do whatever dance you're in the mood for?"

"Real tough guy, huh?"

"I'm not the one with something to prove here, but you seem like you want to take it out on somebody. So I'm giving you a chance to make that happen, with no arrests. If you're more than just talk, you'll do it. Otherwise, you got nothing to say."

"I'll say whatever—"

"Pelletier, what are you doing?" McClaren's voice was sharp.

The uniform lowered his head, his mouth set in a line. "Nothing, Lieutenant."

"Then go do it somewhere else."

"Sir." The cop walked away. I shrugged at McClaren, who looked disgusted.

"I can't even let you alone to take a piss?"

"When some clown comes at me, why is it always my fault?"

"Jesus, you really are a shit magnet. Let's go back in the room."

We sat in the interrogation room, and McClaren looked at me. "What do you know about fugo poisoning?"

"You saying that's what killed Kenishi?"

"Just answer the question. For once."

"It's a poisonous puffer fish the Japanese like as a delicacy. It has to be prepared to very exact standards by a pro chef. If they miss and nick the poison gland, *bam*, no dessert."

"Ever try it?"

"Once, when I was younger. Numbs your mouth a little. It was nothing special, just the thrill of the risk of dying."

"You speak a little Japanese, huh?"

"How'd you hear about that?"

"I'm a cop, remember?"

"What I speak is mostly dirty words and a few basic phrases. Hold on. You're not still thinking I had something to do with this, are you?"

"It's unlikely, but not outside the realm of possibility. You speak a little Japanese, and there's still that run-in you had with him."

"If I killed all the people I had run-ins with—"

"I know, we'd be up to our ears in bodies. But maybe you went to Kenishi's trailer with the fish, gave it to him like a peace offering, that kind of thing."

"And where the hell would I get fugo? Did I have some up my sleeve in case I had to kill some random hungry Japanese guy?"

"We found a container bag in the trash can. Must have been shipped overnight."

"From Japan?"

"Well, it sure wasn't from Shop 'N Save. We're running it down now."

"This day just gets weirder and weirder."

"Tell me about it."

"So can I go now?"

"Sure. See how long you can stay out of trouble."

"Yeah. And I'll let you know if I see any itinerant fugo sellers."

CHAPTER 13

When I finally returned to my dojo, I was beat. The smell of the freshly-painted walls got to me, reminding me of all the time and elbow grease I'd put in to make this place a shiny new thing of value, only to have it snatched away. It seemed like my life, where I'd tried to turn it around, and worked so hard to have something better. But others were trying to take all that away, too. Maybe I just wasn't meant to have an honest life, where hard work and good intentions made a difference.

The ring of the phone interrupted my pity party. I went into the office and answered it. "Yeah."

"Freddy Barmakian here. I'm the attorney J.C. called to look into your little problem with a rental place."

I sat down. "Did you find something already?"

"Well, it's good news and bad news, like the old joke. The good news is yes, we know why you can't rent a place."

"What's the bad news?"

"Same answer. If you wanted to rent property, you pissed off the wrong person. The name Richard Stone mean anything to you?"

I put my fist to my forehead. "That asshole is behind this?" Yeah, the name meant something. He was a real estate developer I'd had a run-in with a few months earlier. I never figured he'd actually do something about it.

"Well, the word is out. Stone has connections to everyone. Property owners, building inspectors, zoning boards, fire marshals, police and town officials up and down this coast. With him against you, you'll be lucky to rent a log cabin in the Allagash."

"Isn't there anything I can do?"

"Not a chance. If you're still serious about property, you're going to have to go to him and kiss his ass."

"That's not going to happen."

"Well, sorry to say, but you won't be opening any business, then. You are persona non grata to landlords around here."

I was silent, trying to digest the fact that my new venture was really over, before it even got off the ground.

He cleared his throat. "Anything else I can do for you?"

"I guess not."

"I'll send you a bill. Won't be much. Didn't take long to find out."

"Okay. Thanks, then."

I stared at the phone after I'd hung up, wondering what else could go wrong. It rang once more.

"Yeah?" I said.

"You made the news again," said J.C. "Your picture is being splashed on all the local channels, in connection with a death out at Fort Williams. And yes, they're playing the old tapes from your last incident there."

"Jesus Christ," I said, gripping the receiver.

"I doubt you were stupid enough to talk to any reporters," said J.C. "But someone is pushing this."

"Our little reporter friend Mason Carter was out there at Fort Williams," I said. "Had to be him. Dredging up what happened before, to try to make a connection. I'll kill that son-of-a-bitch."

"I didn't hear that, even though I applaud the sentiment. What happened out there, anyway?"

I gave J.C. a quick rundown of the events of the day.

"You're like a human hurricane," he said.

"I had nothing to do with it."

There was a sigh on the other end. "Freddy called me, told me what he'd found. He get hold of you yet?"

"Just got off the line with him. I am swimming in a sea of shit."

"Well, at least you know it can't get any worse."

The front door of my dojo banged open, and Danny Thibodeaux charged in, his face a mask of rage. When a six-foot-four psychotic Black Belt comes in looking like that, you should probably run, or shoot him. And I didn't have a gun.

"Guess what?" I said. "It just got worse."

"You sonofabitching ratfuck," Thibodeaux shouted.

"Who's that?" J.C.'s voice sounded faint as the blood pounded in my ears. "Another fan of yours?"

"Thibodeaux," I sighed.

"What's he want?" J.C. said.

"I don't know, I'll ask him." I looked at Thibodeaux as I stood up. "What do you want?"

"What do I want?" He was yelling. "You prick, you go behind my back, mess up my movie deal—"

"Whoa, whoa," I said. "I didn't mess up anything for you."

"The hell you didn't. It's all over the news about you being out there."

I spoke into the receiver. "Another news fan." Then I spoke to Thibodeaux. "For the record, they called me. I was fired by lunchtime, and as I was leaving, we found the body."

"That was supposed to be my shot. My ticket. They said they'd call me. Instead, your face is all over the news."

"Well, I'm done with that."

"If you fucked this up for me, I swear to god, I'll destroy you." Thibodeaux looked around for something to pulverize, and sidekicked a wastebasket, sending the contents flying. I couldn't get mad, because he was just a child having a tantrum. And now I knew what it was like to have your dream stolen from you.

"I told you, I'm done. I've had enough fun for one day. There's a lot of money tied up in production, so they'll probably continue shooting after things calm down. Call them again."

"You better not be lying to me."

"Scout's honor." I put up my three fingers in salute.

"Why you doing this to me? Is it because I've got a successful studio, and you're stuck with this shithole?"

It was like he'd slapped me. All I'd done to this place, and he acts as if it wasn't different? All caution and playing nice went out the window with that remark. "Talk to you later," I said, and hung up the phone. I looked at Thibodeaux. "Want to know why they don't call you? I even suggested they do it, and they told me how you went there demanding an acting role."

Terrified of what he was about to hear, his eyes were like those of a frightened horse.

"They said you couldn't act. But you were such as asshole they didn't want you around for anything else. You're the one who blew your chance."

"You're a fucking liar!"

"So why don't they call you then, huh? It's not me. They don't call you because they don't want you, and they never will. You did this to yourself, like you always do."

Thibodeaux stiffened as if struck, then his shoulders sagged and his mouth went slack. The anger was gone from his eyes, replaced with a haunted look. He turned his back and left, without another word.

I watched him go, feeling at first like I'd got him good. Then I realized how I'd sunk to his level, and was ashamed of myself. He'd wounded my pride, so I went after him to take his away. It's a terrible thing to strip away a man's illusions about himself.

I sat with my head in my hands. The front door opened again, and in walked Spiky-hair and Ponytail.

"Hope that Thibodeaux guy didn't give you a hard time," Ponytail said. "We saw him coming in, and had to hide so he wouldn't see us."

"Actually, he did give me a hard time," I said. "He's pissed that you guys wouldn't hire him, but he blames me for working with you. What do you guys want, anyway?"

"Mr. Harada wants to see you. He'd like you to be his guest for dinner."

Dale T. Phillips

CHAPTER 14

Ponytail and Spiky-hair dropped me off at the dock, by a waiting speedboat with a Japanese driver who didn't speak English, or at least pretended not to. We roared off for Harada's private island, going too fast, which made for mighty rough going. From the way the driver took us straight over the waves, he might have been a kamikaze pilot in a former life.

Spray blew onto me every time we smacked down, and my thoughts were bouncing around as much as I was. We hit a big swell and came down hard. The driver turned back to check on me, maybe worried that he'd bounced me out. He eased back on the throttle, and as we slowed, the ride got less choppy. I was glad he'd come to his senses, or maybe he'd realized it wouldn't do to drown his bosses' dinner guest.

There were a number of islands in Casco Bay, and when we got past Peak's, the big one, the driver threaded through the buoys blinking in the fading light of sunset. I didn't know how things were going to go with Harada, or what I would say to him, so I started thinking up questions. It was almost dark when the boat finally pulled up to a dock. The island itself was just an indistinct shadow in the gloom, but there lights on the dock, and at various points up a path. The glow of more light came from behind a rise.

I stepped out onto the planks, as another Japanese man on the dock bowed to me before tying up the boat. He motioned for me to follow him, and we walked up an illuminated gravel path, the stones crunching underfoot. We went up the small rise, and I saw a wire fence that stretched in either direction. The top of the fence had coils of razor wire. I stopped and looked at my escort. What kind of place was this, a government lab? Was Harada running secret experiments, or playing *Dr. No* out here in the harbor? I wasn't in the mood to be James Bond, and was getting agitated. My escort motioned me onward, and I saw the gun clipped to his belt holster. This was looking more and more like a bad idea.

We walked on until we came to a gate, guarded by another man, who wore a windbreaker over black pants and polo shirt. He also had a pistol clipped to his belt. The dock guy nodded to the gate guard, who spoke rapid Japanese into a walkie-talkie before letting us through. Now I was thoroughly spooked.

The house was a rambling Victorian monstrosity, which surprised me. After all the security I'd gone through, I kind of expected a modern fortress, or some sort of bunker. But it was just your typical old-money Maine island house, albeit on the larger side, and with enough floodlights to keep a field of illumination all around the perimeter.

We went up to the front door, and my guide knocked. The door was opened by another Japanese man in a suit-coat and tie. He was also packing a gun, in a shoulder rig under the suit-coat.

My dock escort stayed outside, and the suit took me from there. The interior of the house was roomy and tastefully furnished in late-model Japanese style, with some traditional touches: decorated screens, large vases, wall hangings, some Hokusai prints. I was wondering if the dining room would have a traditional low table and mats to kneel on, but when we came to it, it had a regular-height dining table and chairs, and could comfortably seat over two dozen. The dining room itself was maybe a little smaller than a hangar.

My host stood up when I entered. He was older, stocky, with close-cropped, iron-gray hair. He was about five-ten, tall for a Japanese man, and just a shade shorter than me. His silk suit-coat was of much greater quality than that of the hired help.

He bowed. "Mr. Taylor." There was just a slight trace of an accent, but he'd had good language training.

I returned his bow. "Konban-wa, Harada-san."

"Very good, Mr. Taylor." There was a slight crinkling around Harada's eyes, which may have been pleasure. "And thank you for coming to see me."

"I imagine this is a much anticipated meeting on both sides."

"Indeed." Harada frowned, looking down at my sleeve. "But you're wet. It was the driver, wasn't it? I told him he is too wild, goes too fast. He will be punished later."

"Please do not do so on my account, Harada-san. It is of no consequence." I hadn't wanted to get the guy in trouble, but as I watched Harada, something clicked. It was a test. He'd probably told the guy to deliberately drive fast and wild, to set this up, and note my reaction. Japanese businessmen often viewed negotiations as a subtle form of warfare, and I was being calibrated. Well, I'd studied Sun Tzu's *The Art of War* and Musashi's *The Book of Five Rings* as well, so I wasn't completely ignorant of what he'd be doing.

"I will not offer you alcohol, as I understand you do not partake. What would you prefer?"

So he'd done some research on me. "Club soda with a lime, thank you."

Harada flicked his gaze to a nearby man, who made a slight bow and scurried off to get my drink.

"We're having fish for dinner, unless you'd like something else."

As long as it wasn't fugo. I smiled, careful not to show my teeth, a crudity in his culture. "That's fine, thank you."

"Please be seated. We have much to talk about."

You got that right, I thought to myself. His manner was easy, friendly, so I matched him, but I was on guard.

Harada led me to the table, and we sat at two places set on one end, with an impressive display of fine china, silver, and crystal. While much of the house's décor was Eastern, the dining room was not. Interesting.

The attendant placed my drink before me and glided away, as silent as a ninja. Harada had a thick tumbler of amber liquid.

"Not *Suntori,* I take it," I said, indicating his glass, and name-checking the popular Japanese brand of Scotch.

He all but wrinkled his nose. "Suntori is fit only for a mid-level *sarariman,*" he said, using the term for salaried white-collar guys going nowhere. He held up his glass. "This is a thirty-year old single malt, from the Highlands."

"I know someone who would enjoy that."

"Ah, yes, your friend J.C. Reed."

Man, this guy had been doing some poking around, and I was getting nervous at how much he was willing to show. It meant he knew a lot more than he was saying. But I didn't have to play defense all night, I could take a little initiative to see how he'd respond.

"Quite a place you have here," I said.

"Do you like it?"

I looked directly at him. "It looks very secure."

Harada smiled. "There is more to it. You should see the lovely gardens in back."

"But so many protective measures. Fences, guns, guards. Anyone in particular giving you problems?"

"A man of my means and influence tends to make enemies."

"You have enemies here? We're a long way from Japan."

"I understand you have enemies as well, Mr. Taylor. A number of them, and you have not been here even as long as I have."

"And how would you know about that?"

The silent attendant approached with dishes. "Ah, here's the first course," said Harada, evading the question. "A lobster bisque, in honor of our local fare."

I raised an eyebrow, and he nodded, as if in approval. "You need not worry about alcohol content. There is no real sherry in it, just a flavoring."

Everything he did and said was for effect, finding out more about me with each exchange. I inclined my head slightly and sampled the bisque. It was delicious, with small, tender slivers of succulent lobster meat.

I fired another volley. "So you came to Maine for the lobster?"

Harada chuckled. "Among other things. For example, privacy is respected here, despite the curiosity of the locals."

"There isn't as much privacy for some. I take it you saw the news today?"

A slight nod. "An unfortunate occurrence. I am taking measures to see that it does not happen again. That kind of publicity is very bad."

"I thought there was no such thing as bad publicity in the movie business."

"Let us say, it makes doing business more difficult."

It probably meant he had to pay bigger bribes. I wanted to say it, but I'd save the crude gaijin act until I needed it. "Other than the movies, what kind of business are you in?"

"I have several interests."

I indicated the dish before me. "Lobster?"

The attendant appeared again. The soup course was removed, and a small salad was placed before me. Blended in with the mixture of greens was a kind of seaweed. Whatever else was in there, it was delicious.

Harada went on. "Building a business empire requires a great deal of effort in many areas. But the locals are far too established in the lobster business for me to encroach. Like any good businessman, I try to go where the profit is."

"What about movies? How's the profit there?"

Harada smiled. "Ah. I do intend to make money from this new venture. But it is also a labor of love."

"So you're a movie fan."

"I am particularly enamored of the films of Kurosawa."

Now it was my turn to smile. "Forgive me for saying so, Harada-san, but what I saw today did not remind me of Kurosawa."

The corners of Harada's mouth turned down ever so slightly. "Although this is what you might call a vanity project, we are still making a commercial venture. In this country, that means Hollywood style, and Bruce Taggart is very good at making very profitable, Hollywood-style action films."

"Why here, and not back home?"

"This is my home now. Believe it or not, it reminds me of the fishing village where I grew up."

"This is my home now, too. But you decided to use my story for your movie."

Harada flicked his hand, and the salad plates were removed. He sat back in his chair.

"How does that make you feel?"

"Exploited. A bit angry."

He studied me. "You are a great warrior, and I admire that. What makes you angry about us telling your story?"

"What happened out there doesn't belong in a movie. That was a terrible day, and I don't need any reminders."

"There is something else bothering you."

"I also don't like the fact you've been spying on me."

"Merely gathering information, Mr. Taylor. As people do in the course of business."

"Much of your information seems to be of a very personal nature. I don't like having my privacy invaded."

"However, you have been in the news quite a bit."

"And today didn't help matters any."

We interrupted our conversation as the main course of fish arrived. It had a tantalizing aroma that I couldn't place, and some sort of rice mixture on the side, with artfully arranged vegetables. I looked at my plate and thought about the expertise required to prepare fugo. I took a bite of the fish, which was delicious. "My compliments to your chef. He is also Japanese, like the rest of your help?"

"Of course." Harada frowned, as if the question made no sense. Then he smiled and shook his head. "One of the pieces of information about you, Mr. Taylor, is that you play chess, and are good at it."

"You do have a lot of sources."

Harada kept smiling. "Perhaps. But they were not able to tell me if you played *go* as well." Go was a complex Japanese board game. At least there was one thing about me he didn't know beforehand.

"I know how," I said, "but I have a Western way of thinking, and do not grasp the subtleties."

"At least you understand that. Go is to your chess as chess is to checkers, and I am a master of go." He sighed. "I must deal with a vast number of issues and complex relationships to make this movie, Mr. Taylor. The people from Hollywood are extremely difficult to placate at times."

I smiled. "Don't I know it."

"Then you understand that I am not a simpleton. So your roundabout questioning to find out if my chef knows the proper way to prepare fugo, is, shall we say, a bit insulting."

I shrugged. "You're not insulted. You've been playing me long before I got here. It's an obvious connection, and not many people around here have that kind of knowledge."

"To answer the question, yes, of course he knows how to prepare it. But no, I did not poison my own security man. Kenishi was working on my orders, and was a valuable employee. In fact, one of the reasons I asked you here tonight was to offer you his job. I need a good security man on site."

I put down my fork. "Me? I was tired from your set today."

"We can fix that. I need you to keep things safe."

Now it was my turn to sit back. "You've had threats?"

"There are those who oppose this film, oppose me."

"So perhaps Kenishi's death wasn't an accident?" That would be interesting news to Lieutenant McClaren.

"A prudent man would take precautions."

"I've noticed you don't directly answer a question you don't like."

"As I said, Mr. Taylor, you are good at chess." His meaning was clear enough, that I wasn't in his league.

I smiled. "You insult me again, yet you want me to work for you."

Harada steepled his fingers. "I can help you in your dream if you help me."

I picked up my fork and resumed eating. "Do go on."

Harada picked up his glass and swirled the Scotch around, as if looking for a deeper meaning in the amber liquid. "Your problems with Mr. Richard Stone. I can make them go away."

I stared at him. "Stone has a great deal of power and influence. He's a local version of you. But you can persuade him to stop getting in my way?"

Harada smiled and nodded, the puppet-master on his island, pulling strings, making people dance to his tune. "And I will pay you fifty thousand dollars for your services."

Good thing my jaw was attached, or it might have hit the table. That kind of money was irresistible. And he knew it. I wanted to say no, but if I did, what did I have but a double handful of nothing? And if he did what he said, my life could get back on track.

Damn him and his games. But I played other games besides chess. Like poker. And pushing back was a great way to take on an aggressive player.

"I might reconsider if you doubled it," I said, feeling the thrill of going all-in.

Harada's eyes narrowed, then he laughed. "Very well, Mr. Taylor, one hundred thousand dollars to keep my film safe. Perhaps you could learn to play a good game of go after all." He stuck out his hand, and I shook it.

So I sold myself for a big promise, but I wondered if I was making a deal with the devil.

Dale T. Phillips

CHAPTER 15

At six the next morning, Spiky-hair and Ponytail were once more waiting for me in their huge black vehicle.

"Morning fellas," I said as I got in, deliberately over-perky. "Surprised I'm back on the job?"

Spiky-hair drove and said nothing. Ponytail had his pail of coffee, and turned to look at me, the corners of his mouth turned down. "Must have been some talk you had with Harada."

"Oh, it was a lovely dinner," I was having fun playing it up. "We had a nice discussion, and cleared a few things up."

"I'll bet," said Ponytail. He sipped his coffee. "Fucking guy out there on Skull Island, playing his games."

"So you're not glad to see me back?"

"You might want to take it a little easy on rubbing our noses in it," said Ponytail. "There were some intense ass-chewing phone calls last night and early this morning, so it's going to be a bitch of a day with a lot of very unhappy people."

"Sorry," I said. "It wasn't like I was trying to stir things up."

"Are you kidding? You're a shit magnet."

Must be the company I keep, I thought to myself. "How often does something like this happen, where someone gets canned, and the big boss brings them back?"

"Too often," said Ponytail, sipping coffee. "Means we'll probably lose a whole day of shooting, because everyone will have a hair across their ass."

"Not a fan of Harada's methods, I take it?"

Ponytail sighed. "The moneyman's like this on every picture. Always some crazy-ass shit they want us to do."

"Are you sorry you got me on board?"

"Dude, we did our part. That's the way it goes. Now you're everyone's headache."

"Gee, thanks for being so blunt with me."

Ponytail snorted and looked at me in the rearview mirror. "Honeymoon's over, bitch."

I smiled. "Yeah, I got that."

"Nothing personal."

"Thanks," I said, as I looked out the window. "Hey, this isn't the way to Fort Williams."

"Damn right it isn't. No way are we taking you back to that set today. Fucking news trucks and reporters have been camped out there since last night."

"So where are we going?"

"Different set," said Ponytail. "Keeping you under wraps."

We drove to Marginal Way, not far from my less-than-pleasant encounter during my attempt to find out who was keeping me from renting a new place for a dojo. I would love to see the look on Stone's face when Harada used his leverage to make Stone lay off me. That would be worth my trouble with these movie people. Well, that and a hundred grand. Feeling a little better about what I was doing, I sank back into the plush upholstery. I might get to build my dream after all.

We went in past a guard shack and gate, and arrived at a large warehouse. The hangar-like interior served as a shooting set, with black skeletons of metal overhead, long catwalks that supported massive lights. They hung over sets of different locales for the movie shoot. Stacked in one area were a number of thin, green-painted panels that would serve as backdrop for a few shots. A giant structure to the side proved to be an impact mat, a padded block for stunt falls. Props were jumbled in random piles: chairs, a table, a full-length mirror, books, a few lamps. And of course, people moving everywhere.

A young woman with a clipboard came over to meet us. Ponytail and Spiky-hair nodded to her, and left without saying goodbye. I'd been handed off, but was pleased to see that my new caretaker was the attractive blonde from the day before. Today she wore jeans and a blouse, and running shoes. Plain and simple packaging, but quite nice.

"Hi," she said, sticking out her hand. "I'm Samantha. You can call me Sam." She had a great smile. I'm always a sucker for that.

"Hi, Sam," I said. "I have to ask ..."

"Yeah, I was actually named for Samantha on *Bewitched*."

"I loved that show," I said. I didn't tell her I'd also had a boyhood crush on Elizabeth Montgomery, who played the role. "I'm Zack."

"I know."

"So you're named for a TV character, and I'm named for a dead President." I nodded. "And I'm supposed to be security or something, but your job is to watch me, make sure I don't get into any trouble?"

She smiled a bit wider. "What are the chances of that happening?"

I grinned at her. "Hey, I've been on the set two whole minutes, and haven't had a run-in with anyone."

"Good for you," she said. "There's hope."

"So who did you piss off, to get stuck with babysitting me?"

She gave me a look and shrugged. "Janelle Cerise."

I whistled. "You're in deeper shit than I am."

"Don't I know it," she said. "And it's not like I did anything. She's been giving me the stinkeye every time I get near Mr. Taggart or Claude."

"Why?"

"Territorial, I guess. It's not like I flirt with them or anything, I'm not interested in going the casting couch route."

"She doesn't like someone younger and prettier in her hunting grounds, that it?"

She gave me a look, and put on a Southern accent. "Why Mr. Taylor, I do believe you just gave me a compliment."

"So is she looking for an excuse? Maybe she figures I'll be in trouble by lunch, and they can blame you?"

"Something like that."

"Well, let's fool them all," I said. "Why don't we sit somewhere out of the way, and you can keep me from making a mess of things?"

She smiled again, and it went all the way up to her eyes. We walked over to a ladder, and climbed up to the catwalk. She moved well, all springy athleticism, and I admired the view as I followed her. We walked a few yards down the catwalk, and sat up against the rail, with our legs dangling over the side.

"No fear of heights, huh?" I said.

"Hell, I wanted to be a stuntwoman," she said. "See that impact mat below us? I'd love to just dive off here and feel that smack once again. But I got injured one too many times, so the doctors told me I'd better lay off if I wanted to keep walking."

It sounded as if she had lost a dream, and I knew how that felt. So I changed the subject. "What do you do when you're not babysitting me?"

"Production Assistant," she said, as a scene was set up below us. Then she turned to me. "Actually, I'm more like a glorified script girl and all-around gofer. It's not much, but hey, it's show biz."

"You like the movies that much?"

"Ever since I was a little girl. My parents divorced when I was young, and I was on my own a lot, getting away from my brothers, and all the bullshit and drama. I saw *The Wizard of Oz*, and it got me for life. I wanted to be part of that magic, where a little girl takes on a scary, unfamiliar world, and wins."

"So now you're here, with all the flying monkeys and a wicked witch."

She laughed. "Yeah. Television, too. When I got to see *Bewitched*, I imagined myself as that Samantha, and I could just wiggle my nose and make things all better." She looked over at me. "Silly kid stuff, huh?"

"Could be worse," I said. "At least you're not Peter Pan, refusing to grow up."

"Sounds like most of the guys I know." She looked at me and turned serious. "Thanks for being understanding about all this."

I looked at her. "Well, I just hate being forced to spend time with someone so attractive."

She punched me in the arm. "You know what I mean. They said you were a real prick, so I was kind of expecting that."

"A guy like Davis on the set, and they're worried about me?"

She scowled. "That asshole? Two minutes after we met, he's hitting on me. And his wife was on set."

"Great guy. I didn't mind taking him down a peg."

"You've got one bad enemy there. How'd you take him, anyway? He's got a reputation as a tough guy. And I've seen some tough ones, believe me."

"I surprised him," I said. "With some confrontations, there's a back-and-forth, but if you move just before he's ready, you can catch him."

"You've done that before, huh?"

"Yeah, I was a bouncer and bodyguard for a lot of years. You learn to watch people, and make a move before they do."

Her voice was almost a whisper. "I heard you found the body."

"Theo and I, yeah. We just opened the door, and there he was. Called it in and everything hit the fan."

"I heard it was food poisoning," she said. "Bad fish."

"News travels fast around here."

"Gossip is gold, I'm afraid." She stretched and yawned, her body moving beneath her shirt. I was uncomfortably aware of how long I'd been away from attractive female company, so I tried to focus on the bustle below.

"Did anybody know the guy well? He hang out with anyone in particular?"

Her brows knitted a tiny bit. "No, nobody that I knew. He wasn't going with anyone on the set, or we'd have heard."

"Any other Japanese folks around?"

"The lunch crew. You can say one thing, Mr. Harada feeds us well. He caters us with his own people."

A Japanese food service. Now that was interesting. "Really. Sounds like I should have a talk with them."

"Why's that?"

"Maybe find out if they serve bad fish."

She looked at me. "Are you a health inspector now?"

"A friend of mine got food poisoning when some people tried to kill him. It makes me suspicious, you know?"

Her eyes went a little wider as she studied me. "There's more to you than meets the eye, pardner." She turned back to watch the scene below. "At least if you watch the news."

"Don't believe everything you hear." I wanted to change the subject. "So where are Taggart and all the stars?"

"Janelle will be by later to do an interior scene. But this is second unit. They film all the other stuff you don't need the big talent for."

"We're really in Siberia, huh?"

"Yeah, but I don't seem to mind as much, somehow."

I didn't, either.

CHAPTER 16

We hung out there on the metal scaffolding through the morning, lost in our own little world, keeping me out of trouble. From time to time, we'd stretch our legs by walking back and forth along the catwalk, Samantha pointing out things of interest, or explaining certain technical details about the shooting going on. While we talked, the people did their work below, reminding me of a colony of ants.

It had been a pleasant, quiet time, which dissolved with the arrival of a large group of people, causing a stir below. Janelle Cerise had made a grand entrance, along with her entourage.

Samantha checked her watch. "Eleven-forty-five. Over an hour late. Right on schedule."

"What do you mean?"

"With a diva like her, she shows up late, making everyone wait, so they know just how important she is. And now it's lunch, so they either have to feed everybody and make her wait to shoot until after lunch, and she can complain, or they can shoot now, and everybody goes hungry waiting another hour for lunch."

I shook my head. "More crazy mind games?"

"You don't know the half of it. Claude is another head case. You should hear the stuff he pulls."

I shrugged. "He came to my studio. Seemed like a decent enough guy."

"He was trying to get you to come work for us, right?"

I nodded.

"He was acting, playing a part. I guess it worked."

"Well, the fact he has a place in Fresno helped some. That's where I grew up."

Samantha looked at me like I was an idiot. "He doesn't have a place in *Fresno*. Malibu, yes. But in our business, nobody in their right mind would have a place up there. If you're not in L-A, you have to be someplace else that's cool, or you're not a player."

"Are you sure? He says he goes up there to get away from all the craziness."

She smiled and shook her head. "Quite sure. I do a lot of research as part of my job. Trust me, he wouldn't be caught dead up there." She shook her head. "*Fresno*, for God's sake."

"He lied to me, just to get me to say yes?" Deep down, I guess I'd really known it, but I still couldn't help feeling like a rube who'd been suckered by the city slickers.

"Don't feel bad. In this business, whenever someone opens their mouth, they're lying. And besides," she said, after a pause, "guys do that all the time, when they want something." She punched me in the arm again.

"Ouch." I was upset at being lied to, but then I had another thought. "Hey, how in hell did he know I was from Fresno?"

She shrugged.

"Has somebody been digging up my past?"

"I haven't heard anything," Samantha said. "Uh-oh. It looks like we've been spotted."

Janelle was staring up at us, as were several of her followers. We suddenly felt conspicuous.

"Shit," she said, under her breath. "Well, nice knowing ya."

Sure enough, a minute later, a young guy scrambled up the ladder. His head popped up over the edge. "Sam, Janelle needs you to run back to her trailer and get her special blue comb."

"Sure thing," Samantha said. She got to her feet, dusting off her hands, as the guy disappeared from view. "A hundred bucks says that comb's in her purse. And when I come back without it, she'll either rip me for being an idiot for not finding it, or pull it out of her purse with a shit-eating grin, and say 'Oh, it was right here all along!' Bitch."

"That's what all this is about?"

"That, and making me miss lunch."

"Want me to go with you?"

"Thanks, but no," she smiled. "That would seal my doom. She saw us together, so she'll want to cut you off from me."

"Is it always like this?" I couldn't believe the pettiness.

"No. Usually it's worse."

We descended the ladder, and as we headed toward the door, Janelle met us and addressed Samantha, dripping sweetness. "Thank you so much, dear. I want to look my best for the scene, and you know I need my special comb."

"Yes, ma'am," Samantha said, and hurried off.

"How nice to see you again, Zack," Janelle said, wrapping her arms around me in a close-body hug. I could smell her perfume and feel the warmth of her skin as she pressed against me, stirring me with desire and need. She whispered in my ear. "I'm so glad I could convince you to come work with us. I hope we'll have a good time." She suddenly released me and stepped back.

"How could I refuse such an offer?" I smiled back at her, wanting to be standoffish, but it was uncanny how overpowering her sexual chemistry was.

"Oh, no," she said. I looked over to see a group of Japanese men coming onto the set. "There's the lunch crew. And I was all set to do my scene."

I looked at her. "I thought you needed your comb to get ready for it?"

Janelle smiled at me, and put her hand on my arm. "Maybe I just wanted you all to myself."

I pulled away. "I have to go do my security thing. I'll see you later." I caught her expression as her eyes narrowed. She sure didn't like being rebuffed.

The lunch crew was all dressed in white, short-sleeved shirts and black ties, and each wore the same black ball cap with a logo on it. They went about setting up the lunch line with practiced efficiency, even rolling in a large portable rack that held a steam table with hot entrees.

Within five minutes, all was ready. The crew formed a line, and soon they were filling their plates. There was also a stack of box lunches to the side, and I pulled out a pair of those and took them to a spot off in a corner.

I went up to one of the lunch crew who wasn't busy. "Excuse me. I'd like to ask you a few questions."

The man looked at me, said something in rapid Japanese, made a quick head bob, and moved off. I went to another one of them, and got the same result. I raised my voice so everyone could hear.

"Excuse me," I said in Japanese. Then I switched to English. "Which one of you speaks English?"

One of the crew came forward and bobbed his head in a kind of perfunctory bow.

"Hello. I speak."

I wanted to question the man to see if any of his crew delivered individual lunches.

A loud bang sounded close by, followed by another. Instinctively, I ducked and turned, stomach tight. Glass showered down, and I saw flames erupting from a huge light that looked like a massive kettle. I smelled smoke.

A screaming Janelle was on the floor near the light. I ran to her side and knelt down. There were bits of glass all through her hair, though I didn't see any blood.

"Are you hurt?"

She stopped screaming and looked at me with wide eyes, mouth moving, but no sound coming out.

"Are you hurt?" I said, insistent. Her gaze came into focus and she slowly shook her head.

Somebody was spraying the light with a fire extinguisher, and the flame went out. There had been no other explosions.

I helped Janelle up, then her entourage swarmed in to console her, and I backed off.

I looked around. "Is anybody else hurt?" I'd said it loud enough for everyone to hear. There was a chorus of nos. "Did anybody see what happened?"

"It sounded like the light popped," someone said.

One of the technical crew was standing next to the thing, peering into it. "There goes a few thousand bucks."

I went up alongside him. "They usually go off like that?"

"Hell, no," he said. "They'll make a small pop if the bulb goes, but nothing like that."

I looked in the light bucket, the interior covered with extinguisher foam, and pulled out a little pile of blackened shreds of paper.

"What's that?" The guy peered at my open palm.

"Looks like maybe a firecracker," I said. "Something big, like an M-80. Probably a couple of them."

"That would do it," the guy said. "But who the hell would toss a firecracker into a set light? Somebody coulda got hurt."

Who indeed? This was too serious to be a prank, but made me think. If the person doing it had been caught, they'd be in trouble, but probably wouldn't go to jail. But if they wanted things to go wrong on this movie, it was an economical way of scaring the shit out of people and slowing production. Was it a warning? I needed to find out before somebody got hurt.

Dale T. Phillips

CHAPTER 17

A sobbing and wailing Janelle was led away by a mob of people. Others ran around yelling instructions. A pair of men with brooms swept up the exploded glass. The offending light was removed and replaced.

Samantha came back a short time later, and looked at the swirl of activity. "Holy crap, what'd I miss?"

"One of the big lights blew up, with Janelle standing next to it."

She made a wry smile. "Well, at least I won't get ripped for not finding her comb." The smile changed to a more serious look, her brow creased. "It's going to play hell with the schedule, though. They might actually need me, so I better go check." She looked around. "I don't suppose there's any lunch left?"

"They didn't stick around," I said. "But I saved you some. It's over here."

"Well ain't you just the country gentleman," she said. She punched me in the arm again.

"That arm's going to be black and blue if you keep that up," I said.

"Sorry. I grew up with three brothers."

We went over to where I'd put aside our lunches.

A voice called out. I looked up and saw Ponytail and Spiky-hair moving toward me at a good clip. I spoke *sotto voce* to Samantha. "I'll see you later. Looks like I might be in the shit again."

"No wonder we like each other."

I walked toward the pair. Ponytail spread his hands. "What the fuck happened?"

I explained how the light had blown.

"Goddammit," said Spiky-hair. Guess he only talked after the morning was over.

Ponytail shook his head. "What'd I tell you? Shit magnet."

"Either of you know any reason for someone to want the production messed with?"

The two exchanged a look. "Why do you say that?"

"Because there was a crack when the light exploded. And when I checked it, there were some paper traces as if someone had thrown some firecrackers in the light to make it blow. While Janelle was nearby."

"Oh, sweet Jesus in the morning," said Ponytail. "Some goddamned security guy you are."

"Nobody told me you had a saboteur on set."

"Keep your fucking voice down," said Ponytail. "And don't say that again. Christ, you want us to shut down? That kind of talk is murder."

"I want to talk to the crew one-on-one, see if anyone saw anything."

"Oh, man, oh, man," said Spiky-hair, rubbing his gelled head. "We got some major damage control to do."

"You got that right," said Ponytail. "The news crews have already descended. Some asshole called them."

"Did you hear how Janelle is doing? Is she okay?"

Ponytail gave me a sour look. "No, Janelle is *not* fucking okay. She's about as far from okay as she gets. She's back at her guest house, getting tranked."

"Tranked?"

"Knocked out with tranquilizers. We'll be lucky to get anything out of her for the rest of the week, unless she decides to play the plucky heroine and come back to work."

"Keeping her away might not be such a bad idea," I said. "If someone is, you know, making mischief."

The two exchanged another glance, then Ponytail gave me a hard stare. "Are you sure you're not trying to fuck with us?"

"What do you mean?"

"All this shit happens when you're around. A guy dies, you're there. A light blows up next to our star, you're there. Shit, no matter where we put you, it's a clusterfuck."

"It's just chance," I said. "I want the movie to go on, just like you guys. I'm getting paid, remember?"

"I just wanted to check, because we're putting our balls in your hands. Especially now."

"What do you mean?"

"Janelle wants you as her personal bodyguard." Ponytail put on a grim smile. "So we're going to park you out at her place. First we had to babysit you. Now you get to babysit her."

"Now hold on—"

"We already called Harada. He said to make it happen."

"I don't think she's in any real danger," I said.

"It doesn't matter what you think. On this set, you do what you're told. She's the star. Whatever she wants, she gets. And she wants you outside her door."

"You people sure do change your minds fast."

"At twenty grand an hour, we have to make quick decisions." Ponytail shook his head. "Although I don't know about this one. With your track record, she'll probably be dead by nightfall."

"Thanks for the vote of confidence."

"Don't mention it. You ready to roll? We'll go out the side here," Ponytail indicated a door. "Avoid the press."

It was a good thing we hadn't gone out the front, because the horde of newspeople and security guards made it look like a riot. In the distance, I saw Mason Carter trying to push his way in through the teeming mass. I didn't want him to see me, so I ducked down out of sight until we got into the car and finally pulled away.

CHAPTER 18

We drove out to Cape Elizabeth, a scenic area on the edge of Portland that had a mix of old and new money, with massively expensive houses clustered along a winding road by the oceanfront. We pulled up to one that had gates set between stone pillars, with a high fence running around the property. Spiky-hair spoke into an intercom on one of the pillars, and the gates swung open to let us through. We pulled up into a wide expanse of driveway that had scattering of pricey vehicles parked in it. There was a Cadillac Escalade, a vintage Corvette, a pair of BMWs, a Ferrari, and a black Impala. The Impala wasn't new by a long shot, and didn't belong with the other vehicles. Maybe it belonged to the help.

The house looked big from the outside, and even bigger once you got in. They had enough room to hold an indoor circus. It was lavishly furnished in art noveau riche, a term I made up on the spot to denote a crappy mixed style of ostentatious wealth display. I saw a lot of vases, shapeless sculptures, and framed wall art consisting of blotches of color that any kid could have made. The furniture was a mix of styles as well, and seemed to be chosen based on discomfort and cost. I'd seen a number of places like this in

Vegas and Miami, where the owners wanted to show off with a pretense of sophistication, but had no clue as to what went together.

And there were no books. I always liked overstuffed bookcases, so I could scan the titles and see some old friends, as well as some interesting new ones. But the place was devoid of intellectual stimulation, unless of course you counted the huge television in the wall cabinet.

We were met by Bernard, the rotund man with the unfortunate fashion sense, whose hands fluttered like a pair of agitated birds. He drew out a scented, pale-green handkerchief and mopped his brow. "About *time* you got here," he said. "Janelle is *so* upset. She's had such a terrible ordeal, and she wanted to know she could be safe. I mean, this is *Maine*, for Christ's sake. This kind of thing shouldn't happen here." I'd noticed that Bernard's fake British accent had slipped even further.

I nodded. "Want me to go talk to her?"

"Of course not," Bernard snapped. "She's resting. But when she gets up, it's important that you be present." He bit his lip and glanced quickly toward the bay window. "I just wish we had access to some professional security, who would really know how to protect her."

Ponytail spoke up. "Mister Taylor here has actually been a real-life bodyguard, so he knows what he's doing."

Bernard looked me up and down as if I was a particularly overripe piece of fruit. "Perhaps you're good at the style of fighting we do in these movies, but what kind of bodyguard doesn't even carry a firearm?"

"The right kind," I said. "At this range, Bernard, you wouldn't even have a chance to draw a weapon."

"Perhaps." He sniffed. "But I doubt you've ever been a bodyguard for anyone as important as Janelle." I felt the condescension drip from his words.

I scratched my head. "Well, I did work for the guy who ran all the numbers and prostitution in lower Miami. Does that count?"

Everyone stared at me. Bernard tsked and took off in a huff. Spiky-hair was grinning, but Ponytail shook his head. "Why do you always have to be such a smartass?"

"Are you saying I'm not Hollywood material?" I feigned a hurt look.

"Just try not to piss her off too much," said Ponytail. "She's the star, and without her, we're fucked. Please remember there are dozens of jobs on the line. Okay?"

"Got it. But Jeez, maybe you folks ought to lighten up."

Ponytail put a hand to his brow, as if he had a headache. "There's thirty million dollars on the line. We kind of lose our sense of humor when it might get flushed down the toilet. Are you going to behave yourself, or do we have to sit here with you?"

"Okay, okay, I'll be Prince Charming."

"Like fuck you will."

I smiled at him. "So if it's this much of a pain in the ass all the time, why do you do it?"

He shrugged. "It's show biz."

As he and his partner left, a man crossed through the living room to go out, wearing a denim jacket and jeans. He had a scraggly beard and long hair, and he sported one of those loose-form leather hats with a braided cord, the kind popular years ago. He reminded me of drug dealers I'd seen, and I wondered what he was doing here. But Janelle's assistant, Billings, now stood before me. "Hello again."

"Hey," I said. "Whose place is this, anyway?"

"The production company rents it, so Janelle can have some privacy. You can imagine the mob scene if she was at a hotel in town."

"Yeah, I guess that makes sense. How's she doing?"

"Okay," he rubbed his face. "She's shaken up a little. The doctor gave her a sedative, so she's resting. She'll be glad to see you here. She was talking about you before she dropped off."

"Who was the bearded guy in the jeans and leather hat? He with you guys?"

"I'm not sure who you're talking about." Billings was being casual, but he wasn't telling the truth.

"You'd know him if you saw him," I said. "Crossed through this room just a minute or two ago."

"I don't believe I've seen him."

"Someone must have, though. Somebody opened the gates for him."

"We've got more important things going on right now."

"Bernard seemed pretty worried about strangers getting in."

Billings sighed. "Bernard likes to exaggerate sometimes."

"So there's nobody out to get Janelle that you know of? No threats or stalkers recently?"

"She gets a great deal of fan mail. Some of it can get a little personal."

"You don't take it seriously?"

"If we took it seriously every time she got a less-than-admirable letter, she'd never leave the house."

"You save any of those letters?"

"They're screened by a service out in L-A. She never sees them."

"So maybe someone wanted to get closer, scare her a little, attract her attention."

"I suppose that's possible."

"Then maybe you do want to get her a bodyguard service. I'm not going to be with her twenty-four hours a day."

"Is that really necessary?"

"Didn't the police go through any of this?"

"We didn't call the police."

"What? Why not?"

"We're calling it an accident, and we're insured. We don't want bad publicity on this. If word starts getting out about trouble on the set ..."

"You're more worried about the press than a potential stalker?"

"I wish you wouldn't talk like that. About a year and a half ago, we had a problem with a guy. Got very messy, and we just don't want the hassle of going through that shit again."

"Well, we don't know if she was the target today, or someone was just causing general trouble. But to be on the safe side, you should get her a bodyguard service."

"That's what she wanted you for."

"You sure about that? That that's all she wanted?"

Billings gave a big sigh. "Listen, Janelle's more than just a client to me, she's a friend. And she makes some bad choices sometimes. I don't know what kind of person you are, but she may turn to you in her need, and if she does, it will be merely a temporary thing to get her through. But that doesn't mean you can take advantage of the situation. And if you hurt her in any way, I will personally see to it you come into a world of grief. Are we clear?"

"I'm not here to hurt her."

"Good."

"Loyalty is a fine thing."

Billings nodded and walked away.

So Billings had some secrets, was covering up for some guy, and worse yet, Janelle might have been the target. That made me wonder once more if Kenishi's death was truly an accident. It seemed too coincidental to have the head of security out of the way just as trouble started. But if it was a random fan as the source of trouble, they wouldn't likely have the wherewithal to set up something as elaborate as getting the security chief to eat fugo. I was missing too much information, and I needed movement to think, not just sit around here waiting for a sedated starlet to wake up.

From my bodyguard days, it was a habit to survey a site for potential escape routes and incoming dangers, so I went outside to check the grounds and get my bearings. While I took in the ocean view, I also noted the ways a person could come onto the property from the rocky frontage. I walked the perimeter, and saw a couple of spots where a person could get over the fence from a nearby tree. And once on the grounds, there were too many places to hide.

If there really was someone wishing to do harm to Janelle, I was going to need a lot more help, and she'd need a much safer place.

CHAPTER 19

Janelle emerged all puffy-eyed from her room at about dinnertime, wearing a gorgeous embroidered dressing gown. Her hair was a bit mussed, and she moved in slow motion, coming to me across the room with a big smile.

"You're here. I hoped you would be." She put up her arms and slid them around my neck, pulling me close to her. "Thank you for looking after me," she whispered in my ear, her voice like honey. Warmth still lingered on her from the bed, and she moved to fit against me at every possible point. The smell of her perfume was faint, but still attractive. I was too close to an obvious physical response, and needed to break the spell.

"Sure thing. Hey, how about some dinner?"

She pulled her head back and looked me in the face. "Is that what you really want right now?"

"Yeah, I've been here awhile, and I'm starting to get hungry."

"Me too," she said, her hand playing across my chest. "But couldn't the food wait for a bit?"

"Low blood sugar," I lied. "If I don't get something soon, I might pass out."

"Well, we can't have that," her mouth twisted up into a smile on one side. "I'll have Raymond order some."

I'd have been happy with a pizza, but that wasn't for the likes of a Hollywood starlet. Half an hour later, a truck arrived with a full meal for Janelle and her staff, and the Japanese delivery guys were dressed the same as the lunch crew.

Janelle ordered them to lay out food in the dining room, and had them take the rest of it for the staff into the kitchen, which had seating at another table there.

"Come, Zack," she said, holding out her hand. "Let's eat."

We went to the dining room, where two places were set, and about half a dozen trays of food. There was an abundance of sushi and salad, three types of noodles, and other plates of tempura and teriyaki meats.

"Would you be so good as to open the wine?" She said it like an invitation to other things. Temptation was gnawing at me from different directions. The sweet forgetfulness of liquor, an attractive woman who was offering herself to me, and my need for comfort all tore at my self-restraint. I managed to open the bottle of wine without breaking the cork apart, and I smelled the heady aroma of the bouquet. I set the bottle on the table, my hand shaking a little. I knew many men would have loved to be in my situation, but I was being tortured by my resistance to doing something I'd later regret.

"Fill me up," she said, stroking her glass. I had just enough control to pour for her, and set the bottle down.

"You're not joining me?"

"I don't drink."

"So what do you do for fun?" She smiled at me like she was a cat playing with a mouse. I was sure she could sense my weakening self-resolve.

"I read."

She laughed, the sound like a brook splashing over rocks in a cool forest. "A man with muscles and a build like yours, and that comes from reading?"

"Well, when I'm not reading, I hit people."

She laughed again, then her eyes went to half-mast and blinked twice as she almost purred. "I don't think I've ever met anyone quite like you." Her hand reached across and took mine. I stared at it, under her spell.

Bernard appeared. "Janelle, did you get the—" He stopped as she shot him a ferocious look. "Sorry." He instantly retreated. I hadn't thought a man that large could move so fast.

The interruption had given me a chance to breathe and reclaim my hand.

"Now, where were we?" Janelle smiled once more, but I'd shaken it off for the moment.

"About to try this great meal," I passed her a plate of tempura.

She looked at it, then at me. Her expression was unreadable. "Why not?" She took the plate.

The food was excellent, and it was almost nine by the time we finished. Janelle had polished off the entire bottle of wine, and kept looking at her empty glass like she wanted another one.

"Let's go to my room," she said. "It's the only place I can get any privacy."

"We have to clean up first."

"I have a staff for that."

I followed her down a hallway to a bedroom door.

"Come on in."

I hesitated, but I gave in. She closed the door behind me, swaying just a little.

"Have a seat," she said. There was a loveseat over by a mammoth fireplace, so I perched myself on it.

"I'll be right back, lover." Janelle sashayed to the bathroom. I had surrendered to the inevitable, though I was still trying to make excuses for what I was about to do. But

111

really it all boiled down to the fact I was too weak to say no. I had no illusions that I meant anything to her, and would probably be forgotten in a month. Hemingway said a moral act was one you felt good about afterward, but I knew I'd be kicking myself for this moment of caving to my baser nature.

She came out several minutes later, wearing a thin, black silky thing. She certainly wasn't wearing anything else up top, and probably nothing down below, either. She licked her lips as she came toward me. My mouth was dry, my need insistent, straining, as I felt my blood pulse inside me.

"So, bodyguard, want to have some fun with me?" Her voice was husky. She had a small straw in her hand. "Want a little toot to get you going?"

I looked into her eyes, which were slightly out of focus and preternaturally bright. And she was sniffing and rubbing her nose the way people do after they've just snorted cocaine. All desire was instantly gone, as if a bucket of ice water had been dashed on me.

"No thanks."

"Not going to join me? What kind of a gentleman are you?"

"No kind at all."

"You have to lighten up," she said. "Have a good time. You didn't have any wine, and now you won't party."

"I wouldn't be much of a bodyguard if I got all messed up."

"Consider yourself off duty," she said. "Have some fun."

"Not my kind of fun," I said. "I think I should be going."

"Don't go," she purred. "After you got me all worked up. I need some company."

"Sorry, but I wouldn't be any company. Long day, you know?"

"I think I could get you interested." She knelt on the loveseat, and threw her arms around my neck. As I was trying to untangle her, she clumsily bit my neck.

I swore and finally got loose and stood up, holding my hand to the bite, which would leave a mark. "I'm very flattered," I said. "But I'm just not up to the task. I'll be out in the living room, still on guard. You should get some rest. You've got another big day tomorrow."

"Goddammit," she said. "What are you, a fairy? Can't get it up for a real woman? All talk, aren't we, Mr. Muscles? I'll bet the boys down at the gym line up in the shower for you, don't they? Maybe you'd like Bernard instead?"

"Maybe I just don't like drugs, you think of that?"

"What? Oh, Jesus, it's only a little coke. It's for fun, nothing serious. Everyone does it."

"Not everyone. And your type of fun got my friend killed."

"What are you talking about?"

"Somebody I cared for was murdered because he ran into guys selling the shit you buy for fun."

"Well that's not my fault."

"Isn't it?"

I headed for the door. She swore and grabbed some bit of crockery from the mantel and hurled it at me. The piece smashed against the wall. I left quickly, shutting the door quietly behind me.

Dale T. Phillips

CHAPTER 20

The sound of Ponytail clearing his throat woke me instantly. I was on the couch in the living room, under a duvet I'd found in a closet the night before. I stretched as I got up, blinking in the morning light.

Ponytail sipped from a cup. "You ready to go?"

I looked at him. "That's it? You stand there with a half-gallon of coffee, and you didn't bring me one?"

"Sorry," he said. "We can stop for one, if you want."

"I want," I said. "I'd also like to swing by my place for a shower and a change of clothes."

"No problem."

"What are you going to tell Janelle?"

"Nothing," he said. "I'm sure she's done with you."

"What do you mean?"

"She does this thing, where she brings some poor schlub home for some pokey-pokey, and we come by in the morning to make sure he leaves, so she doesn't have to face him."

"Seriously?" These people were definitely nuts. "Just for the record, there was no pokey-pokey."

He shrugged. "Doesn't matter. It's one night only, win or lose."

I thought I'd won by not playing.

A few minutes later, Spiky-hair and Ponytail dropped me off at my room, and went off to get me breakfast from the diner down the street while I showered and changed. I got back in the vehicle, feeling much better, and Ponytail handed me a Styrofoam container with a pair of breakfast sandwiches in it. Most importantly, he gave me a cup of steaming black coffee, aromatic and hot. I ate and drank, trying not to spill anything, while Spiky-hair drove.

"Let me guess," I said, between bites. "We're not going back to the warehouse."

"Hope you don't fuck anything up today," said Ponytail. "We're running out of sites."

Spiky-hair snorted. I was glad we could finally amuse him.

We parked on the street down by Deering Oaks Park, a big green space open to the public. Part of the park was cordoned off for the movie crew, and we made our way over to where they were shooting.

I recognized a familiar face. "Theo. How's it going?"

Theo stuck his fist out for a bump. "Not bad. Kind of surprised to see you here."

"What, because I'm the king of bad publicity?"

"The news guys were in a frenzy to get to you." Theo smiled.

"What about you? You found him with me."

"Yeah, now they think I'm your enforcer or something. They're careful about what they hint at, but it's obvious if you read between the lines."

"Sorry about that. I didn't know they'd associate you with my shady past."

Theo shrugged. "No big deal. So many reporters around, they moved me here instead. Didn't want to fire me, because then I would have talked to the press."

"Well hey there," said Samantha as she came up to us. "Theo. Mr. Taylor."

"Hear that, Theo?" I smiled. "Guess you know her, I just met her yesterday. We hit it off, and she was punching me in the arm. Today it's Mr. Taylor."

"That was before you dumped me to boff our star."

"A command performance that didn't happen," I said. "I was out there last night, but slept on the couch."

"Then how'd you get that hickey?"

"Ah, shit," I said, fingering the mark. "She got a bite in before I could run."

"Poor baby. How could you pass up all that wonderful?"

"I decided it wasn't all that wonderful."

"Well, good to know you can still blush, at least."

I looked at Theo, who was grinning broadly. "What?"

"You two crack me up," Theo said.

"Glad we could amuse you," I said. I turned to Samantha. "How'd you make out?"

"Great," she said. "I missed getting reamed for not finding her comb, and she almost gets her hair on fire. You should have thrown a glass of water on her, and she'd have melted. Instead, she goes all diva and makes a dramatic exit."

"To be fair, it was pretty scary."

"Don't you dare defend her." She punched my arm, hard enough to hurt.

"Well, speak of the devil," Theo said. We all looked, and here came the cavalcade, Janelle Cerise and company.

Samantha checked her watch. "Holy cow, I don't think she's ever been on set this early." She looked at me. "What did you do to her?"

I shrugged.

Samantha sighed. "Well, let's go see what fresh hell she's got in store for us today." She walked toward the tumult.

Theo chuckled. "Sam likes you."

"I'd hate to see what would happen if she didn't."

"She's good people. One of the few around here."

Theo and I wandered over to the action, and waited while the second unit director conferred with his people on what to shoot. Janelle's arrival had probably disrupted everything again, because now they'd have to reschedule around her.

Janelle spotted me and hailed me in a loud voice. "Zack. Hello, my dear. Come talk to me."

"Wish me luck," I said to Theo, and walked over.

Janelle greeted me with an open-mouth deep kiss. Despite my dislike of her, it was still pretty stimulating. She pulled back and fingered the bite mark she'd put on me.

"Oh, dear, I'm afraid we got a little carried away last night," her voice was louder than normal, and I noticed that it seemed like people were listening. "It was a lot of fun, dearie, and you were a stallion, but I'm afraid we can't make it a regular thing. I hope you understand." She patted my cheek and moved off, leaving me standing there wondering what had happened. Samantha sidled up next to me.

I looked at her. "What was that all about?"

She laughed. "Now everyone on the set thinks you boffed her, and she dumped you."

"But nothing happened. Why would she do that?"

"Perception is everything, dearie. And now that she's marked her territory, you're her former property, cast aside. Damaged goods for anyone else looking to scoop you up."

"All that for a power trip?"

"Yup. Looks I have to settle for scraps."

She walked away, and I smacked myself in the head.

Just another day in crazyland.

CHAPTER 21

It was a beautiful Spring morning, but as the day progressed, it got unseasonably hot and muggy, until it was like a steambath. Most people peeled off whatever extra clothing they could.

That was why I noticed him, the Japanese man in a suit, standing off to the side by himself, underneath some trees. He didn't look like part of the lunch crew. Maybe he just liked martial arts movies. But I was starting to get antsy about people hanging around who I didn't know. Hey, I was supposed to be security now, and odd things were happening. So I went in a wide arc around the shoot, coming up behind him.

He somehow sensed me while I was more than twenty feet away, and I hadn't been making any noise. Impressive. He didn't turn around, and didn't move, except for a slight lift of his head, but he knew I was there. Not a lot of people on the street had that kind of radar.

I strolled up alongside him. "How's it going?"

He didn't look at me or speak.

"I said, how's it going?" I was being loud and rude. He turned to look at me with an arrogance and disdain that you could have bottled and sold to power CEOs. Then he forced

119

a smile that was more like a grimace. He shook his head and shrugged.

I wanted to goad him into a reaction. "No speakee Engrish, huh? Too bad." He turned back to look at the action. I thought of a phrase that would have made a Ginza prostitute blush, and spoke it to him in pretty bad Japanese. The only thing that moved was a twitching muscle along his jaw. He didn't show anything else, but inside, I could tell he was seething.

"Got that one, didn't you? Feel like talking to me now?"

He turned to stare at me with hate and menace rolling off him like the sweat that soaked him. Why would he stay all buttoned up in this weather? Then it came to me. Maybe because underneath his suit, his short-sleeved shirt would reveal his Yakuza gangster tattoos. The Yakuza were hard-core criminal gangs that plagued Japan, tight-knit, powerful, and deadly. He was definitely the type, and I really wanted a conversation with him. But he wouldn't talk to me.

I needed a uniformed guard, because one thing the Japanese did respond to was authority. I decided against Theo, because some Japanese are incredibly racist, and a guy who had given me such attitude would likely do even worse to a black man. But a white uniformed guard would be someone he'd have to talk to, or get escorted off the set. Maybe he had protection, but I wanted to know whose boy he was.

Nearby, I saw one of the other guards I recognized and called over. "Hey. Gabe, isn't it?" The guy turned around from where he'd been watching the action.

"Yes sir?"

"Can you come here, please?"

As he walked over, I could tell Gabe was in his mid-thirties, in reasonably good shape.

"What's up?"

"This guy here won't talk to me, but he'll talk to you."

Gabe looked at him and shrugged. "Maybe he doesn't speak English."

"Oh, he understands, all right. But he doesn't want to let me know who he's working for. If you ask to see his papers, he'll have to show you. Or you can kick him off the set, but I think he wants to stay."

Another couple was taking in the view, about a dozen feet away. The boy nudged the girl and nodded toward us. They watched to see what would happen.

My Japanese friend tensed up a little.

"Excuse me sir, but do you have some ID?" Gabe spoke to the man.

The man shook his head and gave a smile.

I jumped in. "You're not fooling anyone, bub. Gabe here is going to kick your ass off the set unless you talk to him."

The man looked past Gabe to me, his gaze burning me like a laser.

"So sorry," the man said at last. "Not good English. Very ashamed."

I laughed. Right out of a politically incorrect 60's movie. The guy was playing dumb for the audience, and to make me look like an asshole for forcing the issue. It was okay, I'd played the asshole role lots of times, and didn't worry about saving face. I nodded to Gabe.

"Sir, unless you can show me some identification, I'm going to have to ask you to leave now," Gabe said.

While still staring at me, the guy reached in his suit for a folded piece of paper and handed it to Gabe, who read it out to me. "Says Mr. Oto here is a guest of Mr. Harada."

"I can type up a letter, too. Doesn't mean it's real. He's going to have to do better than that."

Oto got red in the face. This was some serious loss of face. He pulled a card from the breast pocket of his suit and handed it to the guard.

"This is Mr. Harada's card," Gabe said, studying it. "Got a hand-written note, says to give Mr. Oto carte blanche. What's that mean?"

I took the card and looked at it. I looked up at Oto and smiled, deliberately showing lots of teeth, an incredible rudeness to a Japanese person. "That means he's allowed to hang around. Looks like this is your lucky day," I said to Oto. "You get to stay and have fun." I reached over and tucked the card back into his pocket, another serious insult. His face looked like he might blow, as he struggled for control. "You have a nice day, now." I turned away. "Thanks Gabe. We can't be too careful, with all these strangers around."

CHAPTER 22

If indeed there was a hardcore Japanese gangster on site, with the blessing of the man in charge, it meant nothing but trouble. Were Harada and the deceased Kenishi also Yakuza? That would certainly explain the intense level of security on the island, and make sense of Harada's comments about enemies.

The possibilities put Kenishi's death in a whole new light. I hadn't really thought it was murder, as Lieutenant McClaren hadn't mentioned any signs of struggle on Kenishi's body. But now I had to wonder if Kenishi had been killed, and been replaced by Oto.

Maybe I could find out some background information on Harada. The Portland city library wasn't far from Deering Oaks, so I took a walk.

As I made the trek, the unseasonable spring heat got to me, and I was sweating heavily by the time I got to the library.

At the reference desk, I spoke with a thin young man and explained that I was looking for information on the Japanese millionaire who had bought the island in Casco Bay. For the next hour I searched microfilm archives from the *Portland*

Press Herald, and found a few items. A Japanese businessman with interests in the Maine fishing industry had been found dead in his car, down near the docks. It had been ruled a death by natural causes, but I flagged it as an item for further digging, and wrote down some notes.

I found another item of interest, where a commercial fishing boat had been burned a few months before, a deliberate case of arson. Good thing I hadn't been in town then, or Sergeant Lagasse would probably have tried to pin the crimes on me. Were these connected at all to Harada and his interests in the industry? I'd need more information, though I couldn't discover anything more in my current search.

The idea of gangsters reminded me that I had another one to worry about, with a more personal tone. I'd been distracted with all that was going on, and realized it was a good idea to remember Ollie Southern was likely waiting to get back at me. He was the former leader of a motorcycle gang I'd run afoul of, and while some motorcycle clubs were peaceful and law-abiding, Ollie's was one of the worst. He'd brought a group of his men to my dojo to beat me to death, but I'd called the cops, who for once had shown up on time. I'd thought the charges serious enough to have Ollie put away for a while, but in the modern system of justice, any crime could be forgiven if you had something to trade.

I knew I'd deliberately put off thinking about him, but while I was here, decided to check up on Ollie's gang. The archives had over a dozen references, with connections to four homicides in the last ten years. I was hoping some kind of clue would appear, some hint as to where Ollie might be staying while he plotted his revenge, but I got nothing of value.

It was getting on in the afternoon, and I wanted to return to the set. On the way out, I saw a sign for a public hearing to be held that night. Ordinarily, I wouldn't have paid any attention to it, but the name on the sign caught my eye. Stone. Richard Stone was going to be appearing before the

Portland Zoning Commission at seven o'clock tonight to give details on another project.

Well, I knew what I'd be doing after dinner. Causing trouble yet again.

I walked back to Deering Oaks, working up a good sweat once more. Wonder of wonders, nothing bad had happened on the set in my absence. Maybe they were right; maybe I was the catalyst for trouble.

Under a tent was a cooler for the crew which held plastic water bottles. I plucked out two from the ice, opened one, and drank about half of it before resealing it and moving on. Then I found Theo, who looked wilted from the heat.

"Are you getting enough water?" I said, handing him the second bottle. "You look like you've shed some liquid."

"Coming from you, that's funny," Theo said. "You look like you've been swimming." He drank his bottle down in four gulps. "Thanks."

"How's it been going?"

"Slow and hot," Theo said. "Lot of bitching and moaning."

"Big surprise," I said. "Where's Janelle? I don't see her around."

"Your new girlfriend? She couldn't take the heat."

I frowned at him. "You are not funny."

"Hey, I'm just jealous. Not everybody gets to sleep with a Hollywood starlet."

"See if I bring you water again." I finished the last of mine.

"Ah, relax," said Theo. "I'm just yanking your chain. Getting kind of bored out here. Thought the movie business was supposed to be exciting."

"Well, it may get that way. We may have a genuine gangster on sight." I told him about the Yakuza. "Keep an eye on him. He looks dangerous. And if we've got someone from organized crime involved, it makes me suspicious of the other trouble that's been occurring."

Theo shook his head. "I was just kidding about being bored."

"Too late," I said. "And there's another guy I want to find, he was out at Janelle's. Skinny dude in jeans and a leather hat, looked kind of like a pusher."

"Long stringy hair? Kind of shifty?"

"Yeah, that's the one."

"I saw him about five minutes ago, over that way." Theo pointed.

"Okay, thanks," I said. I started walking in the direction he'd indicated.

"Hey, wait up," he said. "I want to watch all the fun."

There was still a crowd of onlookers at the edge of the park, and I scanned the faces. A few minute later I spotted the guy, and moved toward him. Some sense made him look at me just then, and he scuttled away at a fast jog.

As I followed, he increased his pace, and so did I. He headed toward Forest Avenue, a wide main drag along the edge of the park. I was about fifty yards behind him as he jumped out into traffic.

I heard the sound of a motorcycle, and a warning signal clicked in my head. There was a loud bang, and without thinking, I hit the ground and rolled behind a bench. I was looking to see where the sound had come from when Theo came up.

"You okay, man? What you doin' down there?"

"Somebody shot at me. Did you see who it was?"

Theo looked amused. "Man, that was just a motorcycle backfiring. That happens a lot early in spring, after the bikes have sat around all winter."

I looked around. "You sure?"

"Yeah." Theo helped me up.

My quarry had eluded me, and I realized I was still shaking. I felt rather foolish, seeing that the onlookers were having a good laugh at my antics.

Theo clucked his tongue. "Man, you gotta lighten up."

CHAPTER 23

I took a cab back to my room, enjoyed a long, cool shower, and changed my clothes. I was finally feeling better, but still shaken at how I'd jumped like a rabbit for a silly backfire from a motorcycle. I ordered a takeout pizza from Pat's, and ate it in my room, my fortress of solitude. I wanted a drink to go with it. I wanted a lot of them. Years ago, I'd tried to drown my thoughts and feelings of guilt and grief, and it had almost killed me. My friend Ben had saved me, and he'd died up here in Maine. He was the reason why I was here. I'd stayed after finding out about his death, and I'd tried to build something, for the first time in my life.

And now Richard Stone was trying to take that away from me, just because I'd pissed him off in the course of an entirely unofficial investigation. He wanted to crush me, to show me that no one talked to him the way I had. But I was going to do more. I wanted to confront him, mess with his head, maybe cost him something.

Dressed in a Red Sox ball cap and sunglasses, I walked the mile or so downtown to City Hall. I found where they were meeting, and hung out at the rear of the room. About two dozen other people were back in the cheap seats with me, and a half-dozen more were up front at a table with Stone.

I didn't know what hell I'd be in for. Stone talked about his project, and the committee discussed it, droning on and on for what seemed like hours. It appeared like they were all buddies, and it was a done deal, so there seemed little point in putting it out to the public. Finally the chairman asked if there was any input from the community. I jumped to my feet, ditching the hat and the sunglasses, and went up to the microphone that had been set up in the middle of the room.

Stone realized who I was, before I even made my opening statement. All his composure was gone, replaced by a worried look. Good. Let him know how it felt.

I identified myself, gave my address, and plunged right in. "Members of the committee, Richard Stone is a crook. He has taken steps to shut down my business, and to keep me from operating my business within this city. He has abused his relationships with property owners, and attempted to deny me a living in Portland. I ask that you in turn deny him this petition, and vote to do no further business with him."

I remained at the microphone while all six people turned to Stone, who grew red in the face. He began talking in a low voice to the committee members, who now looked distinctly uncomfortable.

"Excuse me," I said. "But if Mr. Stone is now attempting to refute what I have told you, it would behoove us all to hear what he has to say.

"Furthermore," I said, before they could respond. "My attorneys are looking into this matter, and will ascertain if there has been any actionable malfeasance, and/or prosecutable misconduct. Any business deals Mr. Stone is involved in are likely to be part of a massive lawsuit, so it would not be wise to involve the city in such legal matters at this time. This is between Mr. Stone and myself, so we would not wish to waste the committee's time with depositions and subpoenas."

Looks of concern crossed the faces of several of the committee members. They had to know Stone was a man who occasionally cut corners, and my hope was they might think he'd shaved one a little too close, and get squirrely enough at the thought of a lawsuit to back off his little project, at least for the time being.

The whole room was buzzing, and the chairman banged his gavel for order. "This is not proper procedure, nor the time and place for a complaint of this nature. We—"

I cut him off. "If small business owners in Portland have no defense against the reprehensible actions of large-scale developers, what does it say about the city, and about this committee, which is supposed to be working for the people?"

This caused another buzz in the room, and the chairman banged his gavel repeatedly. "If this room does not come to order, we will close this meeting!"

The room eventually quieted, and the chairman pointed his gavel at me. "Your comments, sir, are out of order in this committee. However, we offer you to submit your complaint in writing, with proper documentation, and we will give it further consideration."

I was going to do my best whiny citizen role. "I have no way of knowing what, if any consideration will be given to this issue when it is no longer in the public eye. I respectfully request we scrutinize the actions of Richard Stone here and now, in full view of the public, before he involves the city in another questionable and actionable scheme."

Stone slammed his hand down on the table, his face a mask of anger. "This is ridiculous. Mr. Chairman, he's plainly trying to be disruptive. Can we not remove this man and get back to business?"

"You can't crush everybody, Stone," I shot back. "You abuse your power, but I've got someone on my team now who can make you back off. I'll be back in business. Let's hear it for the little guy!"

"This meeting is adjourned!" The chairman banged his gavel to no avail.

Stone was glaring at me, his face red with anger. I'd never expected to get very far, but maybe I could scrounge up some kind of official complaint. I'd have J.C.'s friend look into it.

In all the hubbub I left, feeling a little better. Nothing like a little rabble-rousing to end the day.

CHAPTER 24

My pair of chauffeurs was waiting for me in their vehicle the next morning, as usual.

"Morning, boys, how's it going?"

Ponytail wordlessly handed me a steaming cup of coffee.

"Thank you," I said. "I'm touched."

He turned to look at me. "So what was all that running and rolling shit you were doing in the park yesterday afternoon?"

"Ah, I got a little carried away," I said. "Maybe I thought I was in a movie."

Ponytail made a sound of disgust. "I've figured it out. You're just batshit fucking crazy. I mean, we see some god-emperors of crazy-ass people, but with you, it's like spinning the wheel every day to see what new insanity you're going to come up with."

I sipped my coffee and grinned. "Does that mean I'm one of you now?"

"I've dealt with some pains in the ass before, but you, my friend, take the cake."

I put on a look of mock horror. "Hey. You didn't put fugo in my coffee, did you?"

"That is so not funny."

131

"Well, can either of you figure out why Harada might have a real-life Yakuza gangster on the set?"

They exchanged a look. Ponytail shrugged. "Because he's Japanese?"

"Now who's being funny?"

"Look," said Ponytail. "Movies are big money. You'll find a lot of people on set that come from strange places. Don't give it too much thought."

"Sure," I said, planning to give it a lot more thought. "Where are we off to today?"

"A street shoot. Janelle's got a big action scene."

"So how come I'm never around Claude?"

Ponytail turned to look at me again. "Well, you fucked that up seven ways to Sunday, now, didn't you?"

"Guess I did," I admitted. "So for punishment, you have me watch Janelle?"

The two exchanged another look. "Most people wouldn't think that was punishment. Anyway, she likes having you around, God knows why."

I thought I knew why, but I kept quiet. We arrived at a blocked-off street just off Congress. I thanked the boys for the ride, and went out to see what the day would bring.

Samantha came over, clipboard in hand. "Hey there."

"Hi," I said. "What's new?"

"Oh, we heard some crazy guy at Deering Oaks was running along the road and then flopped down like he'd been shot. Scared some motorists, but we told them it was all part of the movie. Must have been some dumbass who thought he was in the film."

"That's a bit harsh," I said.

"Think so?" She smiled.

"So what's up today?"

"Janelle's character is supposed to fall from a collapsing fire escape. Going to be hell, because she doesn't like heights, or getting her hands dirty."

"So I finally get to see her act?"

"We can dream," she said.

An older man came over. "Sam, Bob wants to see you."

I looked at her. "Who's Bob?"

"Second unit director. I wonder what's up."

We walked over to a knot of people, who parted to let Samantha in. Janelle was there, and she flashed me a wicked smile. "Samantha, sweetheart," she purred. "You're so lucky. You get to be me for the day."

Bob the director spoke up. "Want to do the stunt? It's like the one you did in *Breakdown in Chinatown*. No impact, we'll just get some establishing shots of you up there, then rig you up on a wire harness and collapse it all."

Everyone was looking at Samantha. "Of course," she said.

I supposed you didn't say no unless you were the star. Everyone seemed to relax, as if they'd been holding their collective breath.

"Super," said Bob. "Suit up, and let's get to it."

Samantha walked away, and I went with her. "You sure about this?"

"Yeah, I can do it in my sleep," she said. "As long as I'm not diving off something, or smacking onto anything, I'm fine. The harness will let me control the fall, make it look real."

"This another head game?"

She gave me a long look. "Nothing but. Solves the problem of her having to be scared for real, while it shows me my place."

"And you didn't do something to make her hate you so bad?"

Her mouth was set in a straight line. "Haven't you ever had someone who kept doing shit to you for no real reason, other than their own fucked-up ego?"

I nodded. "Yeah, I guess I understand."

She handed me her clipboard. "Put this someplace safe. I have to go look like my favorite actress."

Samantha came back from makeup and wardrobe some time later, wearing the same outfit as Janelle, and wearing a wig, that, from a distance, made it hard to tell it wasn't the star herself.

"I think I prefer you as yourself," I said.

"Thanks," she said. "I actually take a size smaller than her, but don't tell her I said that."

The crew was shooting Janelle running through an alley. That took about an hour. Then Janelle was supposed to sprint from the alley and jump into a car that screeched to a halt to let her in. That took the rest of the morning.

The crew broke for lunch when Harada's service came by, and I found Samantha again. "So why'd you have to get all ready to go, when they weren't going to shoot it for hours?"

She smiled sadly. "All part of the game."

"This what you really want to do?"

"I thought it was," she said. "There are days when I wouldn't mind driving some kids to soccer practice, though. That is, the ones I'd have if I wasn't living this life of glamor."

I kept quiet, and she looked at me. "What about you? Any kiddies in your future?"

I shook my head. "Not with my messed-up life."

"That doesn't stop some people," she said. "Take Janelle. Three kids: one in jail, one OD'd on heroin last year, and one won't talk to her."

"What kind of a life is that?"

"I do know that if I have kids, I'm going to do it right. They sure as hell won't be raised in L-A."

We finished our lunch, then stood around some more. Someone said they were coming up with new dialogue, and there were a few groans. I guessed that meant more delays.

It was after three o'clock when they were finally ready for Samantha's scenes. Two women descended on her to give her a fresh layer of makeup and overall adjustment, and everyone took places. She was just going up to get establishing shots, then she'd come back down and rig up the harness for the stunt.

Samantha jumped up to grab the fire escape, and nimbly scampered up the black metal zigzag, until she was on the walkway on the third floor. The cameras rolled as they got shots of her emerging from the third floor apartment window onto the escape, and some other ones of her doing long-range reaction shots.

All seemed to be going well, but suddenly there was a harsh metallic screeching, and then a scream from somewhere on the ground, then shouting. I looked up in horror as the fire escape tore loose from the wall of the building and collapsed into a twisted pile of wreckage.

Samantha had leapt from the falling deathtrap to grab the ledge of the building, but her grip wasn't secure, and she fell.

I ran to her as she hit the ground and rolled, but her head struck a piece of metal. By the time I got to her, she was unconscious, blood flowing from a gash in her head.

Dale T. Phillips

CHAPTER 25

The hospital at Maine Medical was an all-too-familiar place, as I'd spent a good deal of time there recovering from some of my misadventures. Although a number of the hospital staff made attempts to shoo me from Samantha's side, I persisted. What had happened to her could have been an accident, or it could have been deliberate sabotage. If it had been deliberate, I didn't know if it was an attempt on Samantha specifically, so I wanted to keep an eye on her, in case someone was trying to kill her.

Maybe I was overreacting, but I'd just seen her barely escape getting crushed under three stories' worth of black iron. Only her stuntwoman reflexes had saved her, and she was still hurt. I didn't know how bad yet, as we were still waiting for news.

Ponytail and Spiky-hair were keeping me company in the waiting room. We finally got the okay to see Samantha in her room. She was fully conscious, although sedated. They checked to make sure she was out of danger, then gave their excuses and departed.

"Hey there," I said. "How're you doing? Other than the obvious, that is?"

She chuckled, a dry, small sound in her throat. "I feel like I fell three stories and hit my head."

"That sounds like it hurts."

"A little."

"I know what you're going to ask," I said. "Did they at least get the shot? Yes, they got it. Might leave it in the film."

"Oh, good. Yeah, that's all that matters. What the hell happened, anyway? The rig wasn't supposed to fall until I had the harness on."

"I think someone is sabotaging the film," I said.

"Why?"

"Don't know. But I intend to find out."

"Don't this just beat all?" She indicated the cup of water on the rolling table by the bed. "Would you mind? Kind of hard with this cast on my arm."

"Sure," I said. It had a straw poking out, and I pointed it toward her so she could sip.

Then life did one of its little ironic timing moments, because Allison walked in, dressed in her nurses' uniform.

We stood looking at each other, not saying a word. Emotions moved across her face in rapid succession. Me, I just had a blank mind that could think of nothing. Like our relationship, I was still broken apart.

"I'll come back," Allison said, and left.

I looked down at Samantha. "I'll be right back."

I chased after Allison, and caught up with her only because she obviously wanted me to.

"Hey," I said. "I've missed you."

"All evidence to the contrary," she said, nodding her head toward the room I'd just left.

"We're not together. I was working on the film and she got hurt, maybe because someone set it up."

"Whatever," she said. "You're free to do whatever you want."

"I haven't been with anybody, wanted anybody, since you ... since we—."

Her face worked with emotion that she tried not to show. "And what about that?" She pointed to my neck, and I wondered for a moment what she meant. The horror dawned as I realized she meant the hickey.

"Ah, shit, this actress went overboard, she was all coked up, but nothing happened, and I didn't even like her." I went on, fumbling for the right words, but ending up babbling. "I'm being evicted from the dojo, or maybe not, if I can make something else happen. Anyway, I thought if I could show you I was getting away from the violence, do something mainstream, maybe you'd ..."

She reached out and touched my cheek. "I want things to be different. It hurts so much to be away from you. I want to believe you could live a life where I wouldn't have to be afraid for you all the time. I wish we could make it work."

"I'm trying."

"Can people really change that much?"

I was about to say yes, but I didn't know. She nodded and gave a sad kind of smile, and walked away. I had no words, no offering to make her stay and think it over. I went back to Samantha's room, feeling all torn up inside.

"Problem?" Samantha looked at me when I entered. "Don't tell me you two are an item?"

"Were," I said.

"And not too long ago, by the look of it. You're still hung up on her."

"Yeah," I said. "I thought she was the one."

"What happened?"

"She can't live with the violence in my life. She's been through a lot."

"Idiot," said Samantha. "We've all been through a lot."

She took my hand with hers, the one not wrapped in a cast. "Look at you. Come to give me sympathy and make sure I'm okay, your ex walks in, and now you don't know whether to shit or go blind. And you're probably feeling responsible for what happened to me, even though it's not your fault."

"I'm supposed to be security."

"Aw, screw that. Listen, if you want to get mercenary about it, this was great."

I looked at her, puzzled. "What do you mean?"

"Are you kidding? Hurt like this on the job? I'll get full disability and a shitload of money so I won't sue. This is my ticket."

"Your ticket in or out?"

"Ah, now that's the issue," she said, making a face. "By the way, don't mind my profanity. The Percocets help, but there's still flashes of pain, and that ups my curse quotient."

"No problem. So you're thinking of getting out?"

"There'd be no better time, would there? I can still have it all, the white picket fence, the docile hubby, and two-point-four kids. Maybe a dog. No more Janelle, no more running for assholes."

"Could you just up and leave the business?"

She sighed. "I think I could. I've been in it for a few years. I've seen what it takes to get ahead, and I won't turn into a starfucker or a superbitch. So do I stay, and still be doing this when I'm forty? I don't think so. There's things I'll miss, but maybe it's time for little miss Samantha to pack her bags and leave the bright lights behind."

"Their loss, not yours."

"Yeah. Listen," she said, yawning. "I'm rambling, the percs are really kicking in. So I'm just going to toddle off to sleep now. You don't need to stay."

"I'm not going anywhere. I'll be right here when you wake up."

"Ain't you sweet?" she said, and closed her eyes.

CHAPTER 26

I was sleeping in the chair in the hospital room when Allison opened the door and came in. I blinked, lost for a moment as to where I was. Allison looked stricken, and motioned for me to follow her. She led me down the hall to the visitor's room, where the television was on.

"What's up?" I yawned. My back had a crick in it from sleeping in the chair.

She took a deep breath. "J.C. called me. He didn't know where you were. It's on the news there." She used a remote to activate the sound for the television.

I watched as a news report told of a fire in a strip mall, and they showed dramatic footage of a burning building, as firefighters tried to put out the blaze. Something about it was familiar.

My dojo.

Staring at the screen for a minute, the import of it all finally hit me. I groped for a chair, and collapsed into it.

"I'm so sorry," she said, putting a hand on my shoulder. "I know it meant everything to you."

I looked up at her. "Not everything."

She blushed furiously, and her lips pursed, as if she was holding back words. "You should call J.C. He's worried about you." She turned away and left me there.

"He should be," I said, but she was gone, and I was speaking to an empty room.

After a time, I made my way to the pay phone and called J.C.

"I called your place, but couldn't get hold of you," he said, when he'd picked up. "I'm sorry. Even though you got the eviction notice, I know that place meant a lot to you."

"I'm at the hospital. Been here all night." I gave him a quick rundown of what had transpired.

He listened to the tale, and when I'd finished, he spoke again. "Are you going out there?"

"Yeah, though I doubt there's much to see now. Did they say how it happened?"

"Nothing yet."

I sighed. "Are you sure this isn't karma?"

"Stop thinking like that. Are you going to be okay? Do you need anything?"

"I need the world to stop spinning so fast."

"Call me if there's anything I can do," J.C. said, and hung up.

I found Allison again. She wouldn't meet my gaze.

"Thanks for letting me know," I said. "I'm going to go look at it, but from what I saw on the news, it'll be gone."

"What about your friend there?" She gave a nod of her head toward Samantha's room.

"She almost died yesterday, and somebody might have made that happen deliberately. I wanted her to have some protection, in case someone was targeting her. It doesn't look like that's the case, so she should be okay now. First it was the star, and now her, so I don't think it's anything personal, just attempts to mess with the movie itself."

She shook her head. "More Don Quixote stuff?"

I shrugged. "I'm sorry. This is who I am. Someone gets hurt, and I feel bad, and try to stop it from happening again. I wish I could be more like the person you want."

"I wish ..." Tears were in her eyes, and she turned away.

I turned to go, feeling like my heart was a broken piece of pottery.

With nothing left but pain, I left the hospital, which was supposed to be a place of healing. I decided to walk out to the scene of the fire, to give myself time to think, and because I'd be too distracted to drive anyway. I parked at my room and made my way through Portland, thinking black thoughts on a sunny spring day.

By the time I got to the strip mall, I was tired mentally and physically. There were still a few people about, in singles and in groups, surveying the damage, standing behind a cordon that some official department of something had put up. I felt myself getting angry at the onlookers. Why did people stand around gawking at a burned-out building?

I made myself look, and it was as bad as I feared. A total loss, nothing but a burned-out shell left where something had stood before. The businesses to either side had sustained damage as well, but mine was just a black, smoking ruin. Cinders still floated in the air, and there was a strong smell of smoke.

Months of work, money, and dreams just disappeared overnight. Even if insurance covered the loss, it would be a long time from now, and wouldn't cover me for what I'd poured into this place. I had an apartment, and not much money left, and very little else. I ran my hand through my hair. I wanted to scream, to hit something, to let everything out in a fit of rage.

A young police officer approached me. "Zachary Taylor?"

I looked at him. "What?"

He stayed back out of reach, hand very close to his service pistol. He hadn't unsnapped the holster yet, but he was wary. "Would you come with me, please?"

"What in hell for?"

"You're wanted for questioning."

CHAPTER 27

I'd gone from the hospital to the police station, and didn't know which was worse. I was in an interrogation room with Sergeant Lagasse, Lieutenant McClaren, and some other guy I didn't know.

"Who's he?" I was in a sour mood.

"Chief Inspector Harold Miller," said McClaren. "Head Fire Marshal for the City of Portland."

"So somebody torched my place?" I looked the guy right in the eyes.

He gazed back at me, unruffled. "There was definitely some major accelerant used. My guess is plain old gasoline. It was meant to go fast, before the department could get to it. Somebody wanted a complete burn."

"Well, they sure as hell got it, from the looks of it. When did it start?"

"Best guess is around two or three in the morning. For arson, that's a good time. Bigger delay in someone calling it in. It was going strong, and no way to save any part of the structure by the time they arrived."

"Mind telling us where you were last night?" Lagasse broke in. "We had a uniform at your door, but no response."

"I was at the hospital."

"All night? Doing what?"

"Making sure a woman who got hurt yesterday made it through the night, in case someone was out to get her."

"Jeeeesus," said Lagasse. "You still have a flair for the dramatic."

"Stuff it," I said.

McClaren broke in. "Anyone who can vouch for your whereabouts between one and four?"

"Doubt it. I was sleeping in a chair in the room, not wandering the halls. The patient was asleep, or at least I think so."

"So no solid alibi." Lagasse looked like he was licking his chops at the thought.

"Hospital security cameras," I said, snapping my fingers. "They'd have seen if I left the building."

"We'll check that out," said Lagasse. "But you could have found a way around that."

"What for? To burn down my own business?"

"From what I hear, you weren't going to have the business for long. Maybe you thought the insurance was a better deal."

"Well, a developer named Stone was trying to have me evicted, and he'd blacklisted me with all the property renters in town, so I couldn't get another place. But I had someone working on a way to make him change his mind."

"Stone?" Miller raised his head. "Richard Stone?"

"Yeah. You know him?"

"Quite well. He's a good businessman who's done a lot for this city."

"He's a goddamned crook," I said. The look in Miller's eyes showed outrage, but I didn't care if I made another enemy. "He was on a personal vendetta to close me down. Hell, maybe he even had it done, after I taunted him at the zoning meeting."

"Figures that was you," said Lagasse. "I heard about some little fracas."

146

"I told Stone I was going to stop him," I said. "Maybe he wanted to do more."

"You'd better be very careful who you're accusing," said Miller.

"Or what, you'll run and tell him? You people drag me down here from my burnt-down business and Barney Fife here wants to put the cuffs on me. Are you even interested in anybody who might have had a motive?"

"Of course," said McClaren. "You got some other candidates?"

I looked at him. "Well, there's one I can think of right off."

"Yeah," said McClaren. "Don't worry, Ollie and his gang are on the list. Anyone else?"

"Danny Thibodeaux. He wanted to work on the film, but it didn't work out, and they picked me. He was pretty upset about it, and he shot his mouth off about making me pay. You remember his little sidekick that tried to kill me?"

"Yeah," said McClaren. "He's still in jail, at least, so there's one down. Anyone else?"

"I'm still wondering about Kenishi's death. Out at the movie set, I met a guy who may be a Yakuza gangster, and he's got high-level access from the guy funding the film. Name's Oto, at least that's the one I was given. I don't know if Kenishi and Harada are Yakuza, too. And there's a lot of accidents occurring on set, too many for coincidence. I think someone's sabotaging the film, but I don't know why. That's why I was at the hospital. Somebody rigged a fire escape to collapse at the wrong time, and it almost got a woman killed."

"You got proof for any of this?"

"No, or I'd have let you know."

"Fat chance of that," said Lagasse.

I looked at McClaren. "If your trained monkey is going to hang around, could he at least keep quiet?"

Lagasse lunged at me. "Sergeant," barked McClaren, stopping him from grabbing me and getting us into even more of a mess. Then to me, McClaren was direct. "Cut the bullshit. We're trying to find out who committed the arson, so help us out."

"I was trying. Are we ruling out anybody from Mill Springs?"

"You mean the ones that are still alive?" McClaren could jab, too, when he wanted. I'd got in some trouble up in that small town, and there might have been some hard feelings even now. In fact, that was a big part of my trouble with Allison. I'd helped her cousin, who'd been accused of murder, but things had collapsed into a big mess.

"If there's someone else, I can't think of them right now," I said. "Isn't that enough, for starters?"

"Guess so," said McClaren. "Harold, you need anything else?"

Miller spoke up. "No, but I want to go on the record as saying I believe Mr. Taylor has a rather overactive imagination and a persecution complex. He seems to think the world is out to get him."

"You ask me for suspects, and when I tell you, you think I'm making it all up."

"Oh, come on," said Miller. "Movie gangsters, other gangs, people with grudges, and even a town? Don't insult our intelligence."

"That would be hard, wouldn't it?" I glared at him.

"True, most people don't make that many enemies," said Lagasse.

"The hell with all of you," I said.

Miller stood up. "I can tell you one thing. If you were counting on getting insurance money, it'll be a cold day in hell before you see a penny, I can tell you that."

I was going to call him a vile name, and realized there wasn't any use. I was just thoroughly screwed once again. I suppose I should have counted myself lucky to not have been thrown in jail.

CHAPTER 28

Back at my apartment, I showered and changed, and sat on the bed for a while, my thoughts boiling through my head. I always thought best when I was doing something, even if it was making a pain in the ass of myself. So I got into my car and headed out to Fort Williams. Maybe I could learn something about what was going on.

I passed the outer ring of guards and saw a familiar hulking form not far away. "Theo!" I called out. I joined him and we started walking out to the point, where they were shooting. "I see they're moving you away from the trouble spots, same as me."

"How's your girlfriend?"

"Just friend. She's fine. I sat in her room last night, to make sure she was okay."

Theo shook his head. "That was some goddamned fall."

"Yeah," I said, musing on whether to drag him into it. "Maybe it was more than an accident."

"Wondering the same thing myself."

I smiled at him. "Great minds think alike. You got anything?"

"Just a feeling."

"Who was supposed to check the fire escape, to make sure it was safe?"

"The stunt crew swears they checked it that morning and everything was fine," Theo looked grave. "There were six long pins that had to be pulled one after another to make the thing fall."

"And, of course, nobody saw anything?"

"Too many people around, no one can pick out anything specific."

I looked seaward, where a foreign man had built a protected compound on a peaceful island. "What motive would someone have for sabotaging the movie? Revenge? On Harada? Is that why he's got a gangster on set? For protection?"

"Gangster? The new Japanese suit? Real hard-looking guy?"

"That's him," I said. "He's got a card from Harada that says to let him be, but I think he's Yakuza. Did you ever see any tattoos on Kenishi?"

"Never saw one. Think there was a connection?"

"Maybe. I'd like to know if there is. Does Harada think Kenishi was murdered, and then turned to the Japanese mob for protection?"

Theo shook his head. "I couldn't tell ya. This job gets stranger every day. I hired on to keep people away from the stars, make sure nobody gets in unless they belong, or walks off with shit. Didn't want to get involved in murder."

"Yeah, that wasn't my plan, either."

Theo looked at me. "So now you're okay with them doing your story?"

"It's not really my story," I said. "I don't know what it started as, but it's not about me anymore."

"And they offered you a shitload of money," Theo grinned.

"And they offered me a shitload of money," I agreed. "Dirty whore that I am. Do you think less of me now?"

"Damn, I just wish someone would give me a shitload of money for my story."

"Harada also promised to help me with a problem. But now I've got bigger ones," I sighed. "Someone burned down my dojo last night."

"That strip mall fire that was on the news?"

"Yeah. I had a karate studio, and was going to have a grand opening soon. I put a ton of work and money into the place. Then a few days ago, I got an eviction notice, out of the blue. I looked into renting another place, but a local developer put out the word, so no one would rent to me. Harada said he'd get the guy off my back. So I showed up at a public hearing the night before last, and tried to tell the zoning board what a dick the guy is, and told the guy I was going to get my place back. Next thing I know, someone torched it."

"Think he did it?"

"Maybe." I shook my head. "He would be a great possibility, but there are a few other candidates, including the head of a biker gang who wants to kill me."

Theo did a double-take. "God-damn! How come you get in so much trouble?"

"I've been wondering that myself. It's like there's a shadow over me." I kicked a clod of dirt. "After that stuff that happened out here, I thought I was done with it, I could settle down and move forward. Then I helped a woman accused of murder, some more people got killed, and the woman I loved dumped me. Now all this shit. I just don't know."

"Wow. I don't know any white guy with worse problems."

I narrowed my eyes. "Are you being a smartass?"

"Takes one to know one," Theo said. "Hey, heads up. That guy you were after, in the park? There he is. See the hat?"

The guy was standing in a small group of people, about fifty yards away. I did a quick scan of the surrounding area.

"Let me get around to the side there, where he has to pass on the way out. Then you go straight at him. I'll catch him when he comes by."

Theo's eyes lit up. "Yeah, let's have some fun."

I sprinted around behind a big truck and got into position. I waved to Theo, who marched straight at the guy, with his scary face on. The guy did a quick look around, and started moving, coming toward me. Just before he walked into me, he saw me, and took off running. He didn't have enough of a lead, and I sprinted after him, caught up, and tackled him. We rolled on the ground, and he came up with a knife. I grabbed his wrist and twisted. He yelped in pain and let go of the knife. I put pressure on the arm and pulled it up behind him, forcing him face-down. I used my weight to make sure he didn't squirm out of the hold. He was cursing a blue streak, calling me every name he could think of. He wasn't very inventive.

Theo ran up. "Nice tackle. Sure you didn't play any ball?"

"Help me get him up." We got to our feet, and I held his arm at an upward angle behind him so he wouldn't run again. He was still cursing, and tried to kick me. I yanked his arm up, and he gasped. I shook him to get his attention.

"Try to kick me again, and I'll break it. If you stop fighting, it'll hurt less."

He stopped struggling. The guy had a face like a weasel, a bit triangular and pointed. I noticed he also had a glass eye. With my free hand, I did a quick frisk in case he had another weapon. I reached in his pocket and pulled out two plastic bags of white powder, probably cocaine. "Got anything to say for yourself?"

He grimaced, showing a gray, dead tooth. "Yeah. Call Taggart. He's in his trailer."

"What for?"

"He's the one who hired me."

I looked at Theo, who shrugged.

One hand on his collar and the other keeping the arm behind him, I marched the guy over to Taggart's trailer, and

Theo followed, after retrieving the knife and the guy's leather hat. I pounded on the trailer door.

It opened. "What?" It was the guy who I'd previously seen in Taggart's trailer. "Oh, shit. Bruce? You better come here."

"Now what the fuck is it?" Taggart's voice snapped from the interior. Then he saw us. "Jesus Christ, not again." He retreated. "I need another fucking drink."

The other guy stared at me. "Fuck it. Guess you might as well come in."

I prodded the weasel to step inside, and followed. Theo came in after me. I was about to speak, when I noticed Oto sitting on the couch. He stared me down, the menace so thick you could bottle it.

I looked at Taggart. "What's he doing here?"

"Never mind what he's doing here," Taggart's voice was a snarl. "What the fuck are you doing here?"

"You've got a dead body, sabotage on set, and a woman was almost killed yesterday. I thought as the security chief, I'd ask a few questions."

"Oh, you did, did you?" Taggart poured himself a tumbler full of Scotch from a bottle of Johnny Walker Blue. Very expensive stuff. Oto sat back to watch the show.

"And I see this guy sneaking around the set," I said. "He had these in his pocket." I tossed the bags onto the coffee table. Everyone looked at them, but nobody said anything.

Taggart swallowed a healthy slug of his drink, and pointed to the weasel. "Get lost. Theo, escort him out."

"What about the police?" I said. "He tried to knife me."

"Guy attacked me," the weasel said. "I was defending myself."

Taggart looked at me and took another swig. "There's no need for the police."

"Why not?"

"Bad publicity."

"I thought there was no such thing in this day and age."

"We take care of our own problems."

I looked at him. "Especially when you're part of the supply chain."

Taggart jerked his head, and Theo left with the weasel. Taggart set down his drink. "Listen up, you schmuck. I got over a hundred people all working their asses off, from morning until night. You think they can do that without any help? Christ, it's like medicine, and it keeps some of them going. You want me sending them out into the streets to buy drugs? It's a service, see? One guy comes here, and everybody gets what they're supposed to, no worries. And my movie gets done. Why you want to fuck that up?"

"That's nice for you. But my friend is buried in the cemetery not too far from here, because of guys like that, and guys like you who buy from them."

Taggart made a sound of disgust. "Why are you always causing trouble?"

"You've got more trouble than me on this set."

"I know. That's why we have a new head of security."

I looked at him, then at Oto, who was smiling now. "You're kidding."

"Well, you haven't been doing too well now, have you?" Taggart stared me down, daring me to deny it.

"You want a gangster as head of security? Wait until Harada hears about this."

"Harada's the one who okayed it."

I looked at him closely, but he was probably telling the truth. "You people are crazy."

"So Harada said you can stick around, you're still a consultant, whatever the fuck that means, but I want you off my set. Go to any of the other ones, as long as I don't have to fucking deal with you anymore. Leave that guy alone. Fuck, leave everybody alone."

"What about the sabotage?"

"You're the only fucking sabotage I know of," Taggart said. "Now get the fuck out of here."

I slammed the trailer door on my way out, under a full head of steam.

Theo found me out in the parking lot, getting into my car. He frowned. "I know, I know. Man says the pusher gets the run of the place, and to look the other way. As long as the white river flows, Mr. Director keeps his people controlled and happy."

"I wonder how long these people would remain happy if the white river stopped?"

Theo made a face. "Probably shut down in half a day."

"Could screw things up for you. This gig might be collateral damage."

He shrugged, his shoulders like the movement of tectonic plates. "You do what you gotta do."

"Not a fan of our little pharmaceutical friend, I take it?"

"I hate pushers. Seen the damage they do. Friends of mine in my school, on the team, throwing their lives away. Lot of guys I grew up with got wrecked because of assholes like that."

I nodded. "Well, weasel-boy will soon be suffering a karmic retribution for his business dealings."

"Some will miss him. Not me." Theo looked off in the distance. "Guy drives a black Chevy Impala." He gave me the plate number, and I jotted it down. "Pusher like that in Portland, I'd try Munjoy Hill. Wouldn't be surprised if you found him there."

"Thanks," I said. He thumped the car doorframe twice and walked away, while I marveled at the bravery and integrity of a man who would hand you a better shovel with which to dig his grave.

CHAPTER 29

Portland's Munjoy Hill is tucked at the end of a little peninsula, overlooking the downtown area. It held the broad expanse of park called the Eastern Promenade, which borders the sea, giving great views of Casco Bay. Its walkways are frequented by joggers, cyclists, and people with their dogs. It was also a spot for people looking to score.

There were a lot of triple-deckers that had been turned into apartments, with an out-of-proportion number of rental units. It was the kind of place the real estate agents loved to spin as charming, historical, and scenic, but it had some serious problem areas. While there were many places in Maine where the locals didn't lock their doors or cars, this wasn't one of them.

The neighborhood used to be mostly tough, working-class Irish families, but now there was a more diverse mix of ethnicities and income groups, ranging from bottom-lower to outright brutal poverty. As in most places of deprivation and desperation, you had the handmaidens of crime, most notably drugs and prostitution.

I got off Congress and cruised the neighborhood, watching people watch me. Those with nothing else to do sat out on their stoops, smoking and sometimes drinking out of brown paper bags, staring at anything that came by. They'd assume a lone man in a car would be a cop, a social worker, a buyer of illicit services, or a clueless tourist.

Since I didn't look like a cop, especially in the old heap I drove, I'd most likely be taken for someone looking for a pusher or a hooker. Well, I was looking for a pusher. It took a little over twenty minutes of cruising up and down various streets, but there was the black Impala, parked on the street outside a triple-decker.

But there wasn't much I could do now, though, other than mark his current location, which might not even be his residence. Too many people were watching, and maybe one of them would mention me, and the guy might put it together. I didn't want to tip him off yet that he'd been tracked down, so I didn't get out of the car. But I did note the street address before I moved on, knowing I'd come back later.

Well, there was always the mystery man, Mr. Oto. I wanted to know more about him and was curious as to where he went when he left the set. Did he stay on Harada's island, or in town? I drove back to my apartment to retrieve my binoculars, and continued on to Fort Williams. I got the same security guard at the gate, who let me in without a fuss. I guess Taggart had thought he'd scared me off, and hadn't bothered to tell security not to let me in.

I asked around for Theo, and found him with a pair of box lunches in hand.

"Can I get one?"

He looked down at the boxes, then at me. "Hell, no. I remember what happened last time I got you a lunch."

"What are the odds of that happening again?"

Theo smirked. "Almost guaran-damn-teed."

"I'm hurt. But no problem, I'll just go get my own lunch, then."

"Shit, no. You stay here. Taggart sees you, he'll probably fire all the security guards."

He was back in minutes and handed me the box. We sat on some stacked boards. "Did you find the guy?"

"Yeah, just like you said, Munjoy Hill. Wasn't any place I could hang out and do surveillance, though. So I thought I'd see about Oto. You wouldn't happen to know what kind of car he drives, would you?"

"Red Toyota."

"Japanese man driving a Japanese car. Don't you just hate stereotypes?"

Theo chewed his sandwich. "So you just follow people around now?"

"Yeah, see where they go, who they talk to. Sometimes it works out."

"So this is a habit of yours?"

I looked down. "It's how I wound up out here fighting a bunch of guys who were running a drug ring."

"Man, you do go looking for trouble."

I shrugged. "Seems to be a lot of it out there."

"Better watch your ass, though, if you're gonna follow Oto."

"Yeah, I'll stay back. First time I saw him, I crept up, but he knew I was there before I got within twenty feet."

"Real ninja, huh?" Theo finished the first box and opened the second. "He sure showed up quick after Kenishi died. Straight from Japan, you think?"

"Unless he was already here." I stopped chewing. "That opens up some possibilities. If he was already here, maybe he talked to Kenishi, and maybe even brought him a little present from back home. Some nice fresh fugo. And then there's a sudden vacancy."

Theo looked thoughtful. "So we might really be dealing with the Japanese mob? Here in Maine?"

"Could be. Thirty million dollars might be enough of a lure."

"Man, the things I gotta do to earn a living." Theo put his trash in one of the boxes and folded it shut. "Now I'm protecting pushers, and in a Japanese gang war."

"And don't forget the sabotage on set. Keep your eyes peeled."

Theo looked at me. "This was a nice quiet set until you got here."

"I just have this way of turning over rocks and seeing what crawls out." I dusted off my hands. "Thanks for the lunch. I'm going to go wait in my car and try to tail Oto."

Theo gave me a serious look. "Don't get yourself killed."

CHAPTER 30

I'd located Oto's red Toyota, then parked up near the exit to the park, and while I waited, I used my binoculars to keep an eye on his car. I waited a long time, and whenever I got bored, I'd watch the boats out on the ocean. There are worse things than being out by the water on a lovely spring day. I forced myself not to think about my destroyed dojo, and what I would do now, but turned my mind to the task of finding out what was going on during this movie shoot.

Oto eventually came striding to his car. No sauntering or taking in the scenery for this guy, he was all business. When I saw him get in, I started the engine and left the park ahead of him. I turned right, toward Portland, guessing that would be his direction. A short way down the road, I pulled over to let him get by me, before the intersections came up. No telling which one he'd take from there.

He passed me, and I let two cars get between us for cover before following. He was indeed headed for Portland, and I trailed him onto 77, across the Casco Bay Bridge, where he turned onto Commercial Street and continued along the waterfront.

When Oto parked along the main drag, I did the same. There were restaurants, businesses, boatyards nearby, so he could have been going anywhere. He got out and started walking, and I kept a discreet distance between us. He went down to the wharves, where the smell of fish and seawater and old wood was strong. Portland still had a number of fishing and lobster boats that came back in the early afternoon with their catches. The harbor was crowded, with the working boats near us, while further along the waterfront were the pleasure craft, and further still were the ferries that took people out to the islands.

Oto wasn't asking directions, consulting a map, or looking at signs, so he knew where he was going. I watched as he hailed the crew of one of the fishing boats at the end of a dock. It was bigger than your average lobster boat, and though I couldn't read the name of the boat from where I was, I could tell the crew members were Japanese, something unusual up here in Maine. Oto spent a few minutes speaking with one of the crew, and using my binoculars, I saw him reach into his pocket and hand over an envelope. He made a slight bow and walked back up the wharf. I ducked around a corner until he was gone.

Now I had to decide whether to keep following Oto, or check out the boat. I decided to let him go, because I wanted to see what was down on that dock. I doubted he'd been buying fish. He hadn't taken anything in return for the envelope he'd given. Payoff of some kind? What was the connection between him and the fishing boat?

After Oto was well away, I strolled down to the same wharf toward the boat. Some of the crew noticed me approaching, and I saw them exchange looks. One of them spoke to a big guy who stepped off the boat and came to meet me. He was tall, about six foot, making him a bit bigger than me. His face had a set look, his eyes narrowed. I could tell he wasn't about to let me pass.

A smart man would have walked away. But my dojo had just been burned down, so maybe I wanted a little rough play.

He put his hands up, waving them in front of my face. "No, no."

I pulled out a roll of bills and smiled, waving them in the air. "I want to buy some fish."

"No, no. You go. You go now."

I cupped my hands and yelled past him to the boat. "Does anyone speak English? I want to buy some fish."

"You go." He pushed me.

I looked at him for a moment. "If I could just speak with the captain," I said, and took a step forward. He caught me and gave me a rough shove backwards.

"Go!"

"Now, there's no need for that," I said, tucking the money back in my pocket.

He reached out to push me again, and I grabbed his arms and sidestepped. I spun him and kept him going, and he pitched over the side of the dock into the water, flailing as he went. It wouldn't be a pleasant dip, but he wasn't hurt, and it would take time for him to get back up here.

I moved toward the boat, but more of the crew jumped over the side and ran at me. The guy who reached me first struck at me with a front-kick. I barely stepped back out of the way. He kicked with the other leg, but I swept past his foot, and before he could recover, punched him hard in the gut. He collapsed, but his crewmate was now in range, and threw a shot at my head. I blocked it with an outward sweep, and sidekicked his shin, followed by a hammerfist to his nose. He staggered back, not seriously hurt, either, but checked in his attack.

The third guy reached me and leaped in, arm swinging. I put up my arm to block, and felt a stinging pain. My sleeve was split open, and so was my skin, with a line etched in blood. The guy who'd slashed me stood there holding his knife ready. Jesus Christ, what was this? If they were willing to use this much force, there had to be something going on. Time to retreat, if they were this serious. I clamped my hand down on my arm and backed away.

But then the joker grinned at me like he'd given me a real good lesson, like he'd shown the gaijin a thing or two. Bad enough he'd slashed me, but now he was going to laugh about it? Anger roared up and overtook me, and I was in the fight for good. I leaped in close, figuring I'd catch him off guard. He swiped the knife again, but I got hold of his arm. I twisted, pulling him off balance as I did, and broke his arm against my knee, like a piece of kindling wood. He dropped the knife, his mouth going wide. I swung him in a circle, got a hand to the back of his head, and smashed him face-first into a wooden piling. The next time he grinned at someone after knifing them, it would be with a few less teeth. I pulled his head back, and he had a glazed look. I pushed him off the dock, so he could join his buddy in the water.

More of the crew arrayed themselves across the dock between me and the boat. Two held gaffs, poles with hooks on the end, and a couple of others held clubs, but they weren't attacking. I looked around, and saw that we were being watched by people on other boats, other docks. The Japanese crew must have figured that they'd done enough by keeping me from getting any closer, with neither side being able to press an advantage.

My arm was a bloody mess, and the pain was throbbing now. I walked back up the dock, and into one of the buildings. There was a guy behind a counter, who did a double-take when he saw my arm.

"Got a first-aid kit?"

"Jesus, what happened to you?"

"Somebody tried to make me into sushi."

CHAPTER 31

At the hospital, a young doctor sewed my arm back up with a row of neat little stitches that kept the edges of skin together. The new gash was matched by the faded one I had on the other arm, courtesy of an enraged crook who'd helped to kill my friend. The doctor was inquisitive about the activity resulting in my need for immediate closure, but I fed him a story about messing around with a piece of sheet metal in my backyard, and so we avoided any talk of police. Best to keep things simple.

When I was cleaned up, disinfected, bandaged, given antibiotics, and in no danger of further leakage of blood, I went downstairs to the gift shop to buy a shirt to replace the bloody one. The selection was limited, and I the least objectionable thing I found was a t-shirt saying 'I love Portland' with a heart in place of the word love. They didn't have any pants, however, so I was stuck wearing the bloodied pair I had on. I also paid an exorbitant price for a small bouquet of mixed flowers and a vase. Then I went to check on Samantha.

Her door was open, but I still knocked as I came in. "Hey," I said. Luckily the other patient bed was empty, so we'd have a chance to talk.

Samantha was watching the television. She smiled. "Flowers! Those for me, or your girlfriend nurse? And nice shirt, by the way."

"Ouch," I said. "Gotta take your pain out on me?"

"Aw, come on. Get in here and let me take a look at those." She clicked off the television, and examined my offering. "Not bad. Thank you. Could you set them over there?"

I did as she asked. "So how are you doing?"

"Not too bad," she said. "No permanent damage."

"That's good to hear."

She patted her hair. "You bring me flowers, and here I am, looking like shit."

"You look fine."

"How gallant of you to say so." She studied me. "I heard you stayed here all night, kept an eye on me."

"I wanted to make sure you were okay."

She looked over at the flowers. "And now these. How should I interpret these actions? I like you, Zack, I like you a lot."

"Uh, well," I began. No matter how uncomfortable I was talking about it, she deserved an answer. I sat in the visitor chair. "That nurse and I had a thing. We're not together anymore, but I'm still torn up over it. The wound's still raw, so I'm not quite ready to move on."

"Still carrying the torch, huh? Yeah, you're the type, alright."

"Sorry."

"Story of my life," she said, her mouth twisting up on one side into a sad-looking smile. "Too bad for you. They came by with a settlement contract earlier. It was so high, I didn't even try to get more out of them. I'm going to be getting some pretty sweet bank out of all this. I could have been your sugar momma. I might even buy you a new pair of pants. That's blood, isn't it?"

"Yeah."

"And the bandage. You've been busy."

"More than you know. Someone burned down my business last night."

She stared at me. "While you were here?"

"Yeah, but there's not much I could have done about it anyway."

"Oh, Zack, I'm so sorry."

I shrugged.

"Do the police know who did it?"

"Unfortunately, there's a few people that could have." I paused. "They might even think I did it for the insurance."

"But you were here."

"No way to prove it to them." I smiled sadly. "You were asleep."

"I'll tell them I woke up and saw you. I'll be your alibi."

"That's not a good idea. But thank you anyway."

She tilted her head back to look up at the ceiling. "One hell of a day."

"Yeah, about that," I said. "Just how wigged out is Janelle over you?"

Samantha looked at me. "You mean, like, could she have set this up, knowing that rig was going to fall?" She thought it over. "Nah. Though I'd like to think so, I'm just not that important to her. She wouldn't risk going to jail. At most she'd just get me fired and blacklisted."

"Okay," I said. "Anyone who really had it in for either of you?"

She thought it over. "No, nothing serious. You're sure it wasn't an accident?"

"Seems unlikely. You trust your stunt crew?"

"Hell, yeah, lives depend on them. So somebody had it in for Janelle?"

"Or just the shoot in general. Would anybody like to see the movie fail?"

She thought about it. "There's insurance on the movie, big payout if it doesn't happen. Maybe the backer had second thoughts."

"Something to check into," I said. "Anything else?"

"Nothing that comes to mind. People were excited about this movie. They thought it would make some money. Action films do a fair amount if they don't suck, and you get good overseas income as well. And it's supposed to be based on a true story that happened here last year."

She must have seen the look on my face. "What's wrong?"

"It's my story. Except it isn't. Yeah, I fought some guys out there last year, but there were no ninjas or hostages."

She stared at me. "Holy shit. What else is there about you I don't know?"

"It could fill a book."

CHAPTER 32

I left the hospital and called J.C. "Hey, you know any fishermen? Or anybody who works the waterfront?"

"Yes," J.C. replied. "You thinking of a new career? It's about time."

"No, I got in a fight just trying to walk up to a fishing boat with an all-Japanese crew. They acted like it was some kind of state secret. One guy even pulled a knife and cut me. So there's something very hush-hush on that boat, and I wanted to talk to someone who might know what they're up to."

"I can set you up with Sonny Hammond. He'll know what's going on, but he's about the most offensive human on the planet. So you two should get along fine."

"Thanks a lot. How do I get in touch with him?"

"Drop by Three-Dollar Dewey's tonight, about seven. I'll introduce the two of you, then you can fight, and it'll all be good."

After I hung up, I wanted to take another run at the drug dealer. I drove back to where I'd seen his car, and it was still there. I did a slow cruise around the neighborhood, looking for any inconspicuous place where I could watch the car. I noticed that the Portland Observatory, up on the hill, appeared to have a line of sight down this street. I drove up to the parking lot and got out. With my binoculars, I found a spot where I could look right down on the car, and I settled in to watch.

"Great view, huh?" I heard the voice behind me, and turned to see a man and a woman approaching. They were older, with white hair, and wore matching sweatshirts with a Portland logo and a lobster.

"Excuse me?"

His voice was friendly. "You can see everything from up here. And even more with those." He indicated my binoculars.

"Oh, right."

"Me and the missus really like it out here. Something else."

"Uh-huh." The man wanted to chat, but I had a suspect's car to watch.

"Well, I guess we'll let you get back to your sightseeing. Have a nice day now."

Though I went back to surveillance, it turned out the parking lot was a magnet for tourists wanting to strike up a conversation. A family stopped by, as did another pair of older folks. Maybe the view encouraged outreach. I was glad the scenery gave me a good reason to hang around with binoculars.

With all the interruptions, I considered myself lucky to have spotted my quarry when he emerged and got in his car. I got to mine and peeled out while trying to get to a spot to intercept him. I caught up with him when he got onto Congress. He drove over to the University of Southern Maine campus and parked on the street. He got out of the car and went in to one of the buildings. I found a spot about half a block up, and waited. He came out ten minutes later, and got back in his car. I tailed him, far enough back so he wouldn't get suspicious.

He drove along and turned onto Stevens, and slowed when he came to Evergreen cemetery. A few cars behind him, I saw him turn into the entrance. It was the perfect spot for a deal, because you could look in all directions and expect to have some privacy. He'd likely make me as a tail if I followed him in with my car. I didn't want him to know just yet, and so I drove on past and parked by the University of New England, just up the street. I cut through the back of the campus, entering the cemetery from the side.

It was a huge place, with thousands of graves, mausoleums and monuments. It even had some wildlife habitat, with a pond, ducks, and all manner of animals. Allison had taken me here once, and the memory was bittersweet. She'd told me it had been built in the last century on the model of Mount Auburn Cemetery, down near Boston. It was a peaceful spot, and people visited just to take in the views. Some folks just walked their dogs, or jogged, but some came here for other purposes than remembrance or exercise.

And now a drug dealer was using it for his business, which fired up my anger. My friend Ben was in a nearby cemetery because of drug dealers, and fury once more rose up within me.

I jogged up a path to a high point of the terrain, scanning all around, keeping on the move, looking for the black car. I finally spotted it, parked next to a van, not far from the pond. I used my binoculars and saw the dealer pass over his package, and then receive something in return. The two drivers exchanged a few words, and the van fired up and drove away. The driver of the black car did something behind the wheel. Was he dipping into his own product? The ultimate stupid move for a dealer. It meant he wasn't going to last long.

After a couple of minutes, he turned on the car, and slowly drove away. I figured his business was done, and was hoping he'd exit the way he'd come in. I ran back to my car, and got back to the cemetery exit, a few cars behind my quarry. I was glad we were driving, because I was spent, and hoped we wouldn't have any more running chases.

Off we went, he leading, me following, on over the bridge into South Portland. He pulled into a Dairy Queen and parked behind the building. He got out and waited. Five minutes later, a red convertible pulled up next to him. I saw the guy do a handshake pass-off, something I'd seen a lot of in Miami and other places. It was the easy method to pass drugs from one hand to another.

He drove to the Maine Mall, and made three more stops before I lost him in traffic when someone cut in front of me and I had to wait for a light. I cruised around for a few minutes, but didn't see him.

Checking my watch, I saw it was time to head back to town. I didn't want to be late for my meeting with J.C. and a fisherman.

CHAPTER 33

Spotting J.C. and his friend in the crowded Dewey's was easy. Apart from J.C.'s distinctive appearance, the man sitting next to him was more than a head taller. His shoulders were as broad as Theo's, and even sitting down, he seemed about the size of a Maine county. He was wearing a long-billed cap and a flannel shirt with the sleeves rolled back to display thick, solid-looking forearms. His face made you never want to give him cause to get angry at you. At Dewey's, everybody sat at long tables, and usually right next to complete strangers. But there was a space around J.C. and the man, as if people were afraid of getting too close.

J.C. had his customary tumbler of amber liquid before him, and the other guy had a long-neck bottle of Pabst Blue Ribbon beer, and an empty shot glass. Boilermaker man.

J.C. made introductions as I sat across from them. "This is Sonny Hammond. Sonny, this is Zack."

The big man put out his massive hand to shake, and engulfed my own paw with a grip of steel. I had a fleeting thought that if he arm-wrestled Theo, it could take a while, and I wasn't sure who would win.

Sonny studied me with wide-set gray eyes and a neutral expression, then put up a hand to signal the waitress. She came over, keeping her eyes on Sonny as if he was a wild animal, and she was afraid to get too close. "Another round, here, Jennifer." He looked at me. "Whaddya havin'?" He had a thick Downeast accent.

"Club soda with a lime."

The waitress left and Sonny snorted. "That's the drink of candyasses who can't handle their liquor. And I don't trust a man who don't drink."

I returned his gaze, realizing here was a guy who pounded you upon meeting, to see what you were made of. "Well, J.C. said you were an obnoxious asshole, so at least we have that in common."

Sonny looked at me for a moment as if he was going to pull my arms off and beat me with them. Instead, he laughed, a booming sound that cut through the noisy chatter nearby. People stopped what they were doing and stared. A nearby gaggle of young folk, probably students from the look of them, nervously glanced at each other as if they wanted to move away. But since there were no others seats, they were stuck enduring us if they wanted to stay and drink.

Sonny looked me up and down and grinned. "Pretty big talk for a guy wearing a bandage and a fucking faggot tourist t-shirt."

"It was all they had at the hospital." I stood up for a second. "That's blood, by the way. And how was your day?"

He shrugged. "So you know how to bleed. What about the arm?"

"I followed a guy down to the docks, where he did some business with a Japanese fishing crew. When I tried to get close, they jumped me."

"You let them Nips mess you up?"

"Well, the ones I got my hands on didn't do so well, especially the guy who cut me with the knife. But when the rest of the crew stood on the dock with weapons, I figured it was time to go. I'll take you with me next time, and you can clear me a path."

"I might like that," Sonny said, and looked at J.C. "He's alright, for a tee-totaling pussy."

"Thanks," I said. "Spoken like a true dumbass redneck clamdigger."

Sonny whooped. Our waitress stood nervously by, a tray of drinks in her hand. "Come on in, honey," Sonny said. "I don't bite. Unless you ask me to." He grinned at her, and she flashed him a quick crooked smile. She set down our drinks and hurried off.

"You're scaring the help," I said.

"Aw, she's new. Gotta break her in. Gets rough down here sometimes."

"I'll bet," I said.

Sonny threw back the shot, and downed about a third of his beer in big gulps. "That'll put hair on your chest."

J.C. was sipping his drink. "You've been quiet," I said.

He shook his head. "I was just watching you two circle and sniff each other like dogs. Just wondering how long it was going to take you to get down to business."

"Whaddya want to know?" Sonny spread his hands.

"What's up with that Japanese crew?" I said. "They were acting, if you'll pardon the pun, kind of fishy."

"Ayuh," said Sonny. "That's 'cause they pull in sea urchins. Look like little spiny balls. We call 'em 'whore's eggs.'"

"What?"

"Whore's eggs. We usta think they was a pest. We'd smash 'em up, and burn 'em when we could. Little sonsawhores were everywhere. Now them little suckahs is a cash crop."

"How come?"

"The Japs discovered 'em," Sonny finished his beer and signaled for another. "Turns out they're like another kind of urchin them Japs is real fond of. They eat the nads and call it uni."

"I'm sorry, the what?"

"The nads. Gonads. They eat little urchin balls. Pay damn good money for 'em, too."

So that was it. "But if it's just like any other catch, how come they treat it like a state secret?"

"Oh, you don't know the half of it. Because there's different types, there's different prices. Like caviar. The stuff the Japs like is wicked expensive, but most can't tell the difference between that and our little Maine critters, which come at a big discount. Some of them suppliers might be substitutin' ours for theirs, and keeping the change, so to say. So that boat crew sure as shit don't want anyone pokin' around down on the docks, findin' out which supplier is buyin' urchins, or how much they're payin'. All hush-hush, doncha know."

"How much are we talking here?"

Sonny sat back with a grin. "A shitload. Millions."

I looked at J.C. "That's a lot of fish balls."

"Ayuh. It's not like lobsterin', pullin' traps and all, you have guys go below and pick 'em up off the bottom. Think they use a coupla guys who used to be pearl divers."

Another shot and beer appeared on the table. Sonny pounded back the shot, and took a healthy swig of his Blue Ribbon.

"There's such a run on them eggs, they're stripping the sea bed, grabbin' every one while they can. Probably wipe 'em out soon. T'aint no regulation to speak of, and if it does come in, it'll be a day late and a dollah short. Just like everyone overfished and killed the cod industry. Might do that with the lobstah's too, 'cept the state is crackin' down on that."

"One boat is pulling in that many?"

"Oh, the Jap boat is the big harvester, but there's others doin' it too. Lotta money, after all." Sonny looked pensive. "Thought about it myself, from time to time, but we're lobstermen from way back. My daddy would rise up from his grave and sink my boat, with me in it, if I wasn't lobsterin'."

"Who do the other divers sell to?"

"Brokers on the docks who come by."

I was trying to make connections in my mind. "And they send them to Japan?"

"Ayuh. Since air freight costs came down, pays to ship things like that. That's part of why it took off so quick."

"So if there's a lot of money to be made, how rough does it get?"

Sonny smiled, a tight line. "Well, you found out they don't like anyone getting near. Even brought out guns one time, when the *Mary Ellen Carter* got too close. But everybody's got their own territory, and they don't mess with our lobstah traps or buoys. Still plenty to go 'round, least for the time bein', and I guess they don't want to queer the deal. They just go down and fill their bags, day after day."

"How about the buyers and brokers?"

"Now that might be a different story. There was some scramblin' for the market when they was startin' out. Awhile back I heard there was a few things going on, some odd accidents, that sort of thing."

"Like that Japanese businessman, found dead in his car down by the docks?"

Sonny stared at me, then spoke to J.C. "He ain't as dumb as he looks."

"Couldn't possibly be," J.C. said.

I ignored him. "But things have calmed down now?"

"Ayuh."

"Like maybe someone got control of the market?"

"Could be."

"Would that be a domestic or imported someone?"

Sonny sat back and smiled. "A fella from overseas came and set up shop. Needed a base of operations, so he bought hisself an island. Little Pine, out in Casco. The name on the sale is some corporation, but it's that Jap fella. They've got all kinds of security, all fenced off and *No Trespassing* signs up."

"Harada. Yeah, I had dinner out there."

Sonny looked impressed. "Well goddamn. You're the first non-Jap I heard who's been out there. They don't mix with anybody else, don't drink at the bars, and you never see 'em around town, 'cept straight on and off the boat. Why'd he have you out there?"

"To offer me a job. And to see what I was like, and what I knew."

"So you're working for him?"

"Kind of. I keep getting fired."

Sonny laughed. He had the glow of liquor now, and looked around. "Know why they call this place Three-Dollar Dewey's?"

I did, but I usually let people tell me when they had something like this. "How come?"

"One dollar, Lookie, two dollar, Touchy, three dollar, Dewey." His head went back as he laughed.

CHAPTER 34

That night, everything I'd been going through crashed in on me, and I couldn't sleep. With my dojo gone, my way of making a living was gone as well. I'd been a bodyguard and a bouncer, but I couldn't go back to that. What else could I do? I was relying on a promise of big money from Harada, but I wondered how much value there was in that. I wasn't helping with any consulting, and I was no longer officially doing security. Harada had me around for some purpose, though. I needed to find out just why.

I'd moved to Maine to find out the truth about my friend Ben's death, and vowed vengeance on those who had killed him. What came after vengeance, but remorse? It hadn't brought Ben back, and the memories of him got more distant with each passing month. Being in the cemetery had been a reminder, and I was haunted by the hollow ache of loss.

And of course it had been a stupid mistake to meet J.C. and Sonny in a bar, because when life got the roughest, I wanted the temporary amnesia of alcohol. I'd gone down that route years before when my brother had died, and barely made it out alive. The atmosphere of the bar stayed in my thoughts, bright, seductive, and inviting, and my mouth was yearning for liquor that could dull the pain.

So the ghosts and shadows were back, and I tried to distract myself with what was happening on the movie set. It was frustrating, though, because the movie people confused me. I was good at telling when people were lying, but in their world, they barely ever told the truth about anything, and I was overwhelmed.

I'd stopped going to most movies a few years back, since they seemed aimed at a teenage-boy mentality, with shootings, explosions, car chases, and brief sexual encounters. Directors were middle-aged men producing manifestations of teenage id.

And the people in Hollywood I'd met had health, money and success, yet were absolutely miserable. They lived in extravagant mansions, with personal trainers and assistants, but had disastrous personal relationships, abused drugs and alcohol, and had recurring trouble with the law. Movie people were not folks I wanted to hang out with. And the ones here proved it, with their endless head games.

I needed to clear my own head. I got up and turned on the light, looking around at my crappy little efficiency apartment. This was no way to live. A short time ago, I'd felt like everything was coming together, and now I had nothing but broken bits of promises and dreams. Feeling immensely sorry for myself, I did some stretches and dressed for a nighttime run.

Outside, the air was cool and refreshing. I got down to street level and took off at a trot, wanting to lose myself in the rhythm and the mechanics of running. I focused on the stillness of the night and breathing: in, out, in, out.

From somewhere behind me, a car started up, and headlights traced my path. I looked back over my shoulder, but the car turned off, leaving a deserted street. Had that been someone watching me, or was I getting paranoid? I couldn't tell in my current condition.

My sneakers slapped the pavement with a steady pace, and as my system heated up, I began to feel somewhat better. A late nighttime run is a different experience. You feel like you're the only one alive, and the streetlights cast an unearthly glow, like you're in another world. The quiet darkness is a good place to sort out your thinking, the jumble and the noise of the day ebbing away with the hypnotic movement of arms and legs. All the problems and questions were still there, but they were pushed back a little.

It was good. It was just what I needed. I even heard a far-off train whistle, and smiled, thinking about all the songs and metaphors it represented. On I went, slap-slap-slap, in, out, in, out. This was life: moving, sweating, exerting, in a silent stillness. Maybe it was the runner's high, or the fact that all the mess was now a tiny speck, far off in my mind, but I didn't want to stop. All that mattered was to keep running.

I don't know how long I kept going, as time meant nothing in this world. At some point, I began to feel a stitch in my side, and I slowed, and began walking, breathing deeply and trying not to cramp up. It felt like someone had shoved a knife in my side, and unlike most people, I actually knew what that felt like. I touched the scar on my abdomen, a souvenir of a short prison stint a long time ago, courtesy of an overeager federal agent. And further bad life choices had led me to my current situation.

I walked it out, and the pain eventually subsided. When it did, I tried to think of times I'd been happy, and there were far too few. Mostly what I'd done was dampen my emotional response and run away from life. I'd been a coward, trying to avoid my grief and guilt, instead channeling my feelings into anger. I realized what it had cost me, which was why I was trying so hard to change.

So in my current situation, I had nothing, but this meant I also had nothing to lose. And so I was free. I could keep bulling ahead, causing trouble and trying to make some kind of a difference. It didn't matter. I smiled, because I had a different perspective now, and no one or nothing could stand in my way. A man with nothing to lose is dangerous.

They thought I'd been troublesome before. They had no idea.

CHAPTER 35

The next morning, I went out to the cemetery where Ben was buried. I spent some time remembering and grieving. Somebody once said that the only people without problems were the ones who were in a cemetery, and as I looked around, that gave me some perspective. As long as I was still alive, I would fight to do better.

Remembering how reading had helped during my own recovery time in the hospital the year before, my next stop was Carlson-Turner books, where I looked for a gift to take to Samantha. I was able to pick up a biography of old-time Hollywood stuntman, Yakima Canutt.

At the hospital, Samantha looked ready to chew nails when I knocked and came in.

"What's wrong?" I went over and set the book on the rolling table next to her bed. "That scowl for me?"

No," she said. "It's just that the doctors tell me I should stay in bed, and I want to get up and move around."

"I know the feeling," I said. "You and I aren't the type to lie around."

"Yeah," she said, picking up the book. "Oh, cool, thank you. He's one of my heroes, you know." She thumbed through the pages. "That's really thoughtful."

"Maybe it'll keep you from getting up for another five minutes, so you can heal."

"Screw that," she said. "I have to get up, get active."

"Anyone from the shoot come on by?"

"They sent the obligatory flowers," she said, her voice dry, as she pointed to a clump in the wastebasket. "But other than the two lawyers who came by with the paperwork, no. That's one thing I won't miss."

"You're getting out?"

"Enough is enough," she said. "I'm tired of being someone else's gofer and getting shit on all the time."

"So what will you do?"

She smiled. "You'll laugh."

"Can't promise I won't."

"I want to make my own movie."

I coughed, tried to hold it in, but couldn't help myself. She joined in.

"Told you you'd laugh. But I've had a couple of independent film ideas kicking around for a while, and just never had the chance to do anything about them. It's why I really got into this business. And now I can do it. I can put a crew together and get it done."

"That's really something. The rug gets jerked out from under you one day, and the next day you've got a great new plan."

"How about you?" Samantha looked directly at me. "You had a plan, now it's gone. What are you going to do? Rebuild and start over?"

"Don't know," I said. "I never wanted to do anything with my life except run away and hide. This was my first attempt at building something, and we see how that turned out."

"You'll think of something. You can't do nothing."

When I left the hospital, I wanted to see Theo and check in on how things were going on the movie. I wasn't in charge of security anymore, but the thought of someone running around committing sabotage bothered me, and I was itching to get my hands on the person who had got Samantha hurt.

I swung by Deering Oaks, asked for Theo, and was told he was on the other shoot at the warehouse. So I bopped on over to there, and found him having lunch.

"Man, all I ever see you do is eat," I said.

"Think it's easy, keeping up a body this magnificent?"

"Must be tough. But thank you from all of us."

He finished his sandwich, and crumpled the paper in his massive fist. "You just come by to give me a hard time?"

"Pretty much. How are things going? Any more accidents?"

"Nah, we've gone a whole day without someone getting hurt. Maybe whoever did it is scared of that new Japanese guy that replaced you. Everybody says he gives them the creeps."

"You saying I'm not scary and intimidating?"

Theo grinned. "Maybe it's just 'cause you get fired so much, people don't feel like you'll be around for long."

"Thanks a lot," I said. "But it seems like someone is messing with the film. And something's been bugging me. I know in Hollywood terms, thirty million isn't a lot for a movie. How did Harada get a top director and a couple of big-money stars to do the film on this budget?"

Theo looked around before he spoke. "Folks who live like they do leave a trail of shit behind them, and someone's got to clean it up. So they wind up owing favors. Maybe Harada bought up the markers and has been calling them in. Either that or a little judicious blackmail, or he promised them something big. He got you, didn't he, and you didn't want it."

"So maybe one or more of those stars resented being strongarmed into working on the cheap."

"Could be," Theo admitted.

"So maybe I need to do a little more poking around."

"You want Oto on your case?"

"I'll do it after hours. Even he's got to sleep sometime, and with all the different shoots, he can't be at them all."

"Could be trouble if you're caught."

"Trouble's my middle name," I said.

"Trouble's your *only* fucking name."

"I'll ignore that, if you tell me about the night security. I assume they're from your company."

"Start with the warehouse, Ralph's out there nights. I'd like to say he's pretty alert, but you'll either catch him snoozing, or with his face buried in a skin mag. If he catches you, just drop a box of doughnuts, and you'll get away easy."

"Thanks," I said.

"You could take him even with a bum arm." Theo indicated my bandage. "What happened?"

"I followed Oto. He's got some dangerous associates."

Theo frowned. "Told you that guy was trouble."

CHAPTER 36

J.C. had the connections to check on the license plate number I'd given him, and he'd done me another favor and found out the pusher's car was registered to one Wade LaPierre, and that Mr. LaPierre had a rather extensive rap sheet, and was well-known to the police of Portland and a few other places.

My favorite method of operating with people like that was to toss a monkey wrench into their plans, then sit back and watch how they reacted. They'd usually have to step outside their routine to do some damage control, and I'd follow them until they led me to someone or something else. I'd keep applying pressure, following these threads until something juicy turned up, then I'd charge in and bust up the joint. Simple, but effective. Sometimes.

The pusher had free rein on the movie set, where bad things were happening. I wanted to disrupt the flow of drugs, shake the tree, and see what fell out. Calling the cops with an anonymous tip to arrest him might not be effective, and since I'd be pegged as the guy who did it, I didn't want to go that route, as I still wanted some kind of access to the sets.

So I decided to keep watching, and following, to see what his patterns were, and where his weaknesses became apparent. It was a form of hunting, and you had to have patience, as it meant a lot of sitting around waiting for something to happen. The trouble was, sitting around in one place usually attracted attention. Luckily for me the observatory was a good spot, as long as I made nice with the visitors who kept coming by to see what I was doing. They'd note the sweeping vistas of ocean in the distance and town before me, and assume I was taking in the view, especially when they saw my binoculars.

Time passed slowly as the traffic came and went on the pusher's street. LaPierre finally came out, carrying a gym bag, looking all around, his hand in his jacket pocket. He went to the trunk of his car, stashed the bag, slammed the trunk shut, and got behind the wheel. I got to my car and rolled out onto the street, and drove the intercept route I'd taken before. LaPierre came sailing past a minute later.

I followed him to eight different places around Portland, where he made brief stops, most likely more drug sales. They were different places and people than the ones I'd seen before, and it was depressing how booming the drug trade was. I thought I'd put a crimp in it when I broke up one drug ring the year before, which started this whole movie nonsense about my battle with the bad guys in the first place. But the war on drugs had been lost, and guys like this still operated in the open, with plenty of customers. And Portland was nowhere near a real inner-city landscape.

LaPierre drove out to the nearby town of Westbrook, and turned into a fenced-in storage lot which had enclosed spaces to rent. It had four rows of storage units, and I saw LaPierre go to the third row in, near the end. He spent only a few minutes before coming out, so he'd either stashed something or retrieved something. I looked for cameras, but only saw two by the office. That gave me an idea.

Instead of following him when he left, I waited until he was out of sight, and turned in to the lot. I went to the office and rented a small space at a cheap rate, telling the guy my girlfriend had just kicked me out, and I needed a place to store my stuff. I paid for a month, and took my car around to where my unit number was. I walked near to where I'd seen LaPierre stop, and checked to see which unit he'd gone into. From the fresh tire tracks in the soft earth, and other marks on the ground, I located it quickly. The unit had a sturdy padlock, but that was it. No alarms, no guard dogs, no cameras. Piece of cake.

I drove out of the lot, found a hardware store, and bought a set of boltcutters. Then I returned to the storage place and went back to LaPierre's unit. I used the boltcutters to cut the padlock off, and opened the sliding door.

Inside was an old couch, a lamp, an end table. Behind it were four cardboard boxes. I opened the boxes and looked in. Old clothes, books, various dishes. I dug to the bottom of the first one and found nothing of note. On to the second, but there was still nothing of value.

Had I missed something? Was this merely a place to store his old junk? I checked through the third box. Under the old clothes, I found the gym bag, same color as the one I'd seen him store in his car. It was stuffed with something. I took it out and unzipped it, and was greeted with the sight of stacks and stacks of cash. Hundreds, fifties, twenties, wrapped in bundles.

Business was booming, and LaPierre must have been making a good profit for quite a while. I checked the fourth box, but found nothing else. I stood there for a minute, but I already knew what I was going to do. The cash was the wages of sin, and I was going to take it for my own. It wasn't like he was going to go to the police. And who helps a dealer who gets ripped off?

I closed the unit door, shaking my head. LaPierre must have thought the place was secure enough. His place in Munjoy Hill was a terrible place to store cash, and he wasn't the type to use a bank for something like this. He'd want instant, easy access, and the storage place was open twenty-four hours. He'd never counted on someone like me following him and going through his stuff. Well, his carelessness had cost him.

I'd love to see his face when he found out his illicit money was gone.

CHAPTER 37

It was after five when I got back to my apartment. The banks had all closed, so I couldn't do anything with the money except hold onto it until they opened in the morning. If you've ever walked around with a monstrous sum of cash, you'll know how nervous I felt. You feel like you can't set it down or leave it anywhere, you have to watch it constantly. Especially if you've had people break into your place or burn down your business. A pile of paper money is ephemeral, and belongs to whoever holds it. You're afraid someone is going to come along and take it. Trouble is, a lot of people will, if they know about it.

So I was jumpy when I hefted the bag and went to the stairs to my apartment. And I reacted badly when Thibodeaux came storming at me.

"You!" His yell could probably be heard across town, certainly across the parking lot.

I dropped the bag at my feet, ready to fight, because Thibodeaux looked like he wanted one. "What the hell are you doing here?"

Thibodeaux spat out a string of curse words.

"How did you even know where I lived?"

I looked over by the stairs, and there was a grinning Mason Carter, taking pictures. I looked back at Thibodeaux. "You had this asshole track me down so you could stalk me?"

"Yeah, he told where I could find you, you prick. You fucking lied to me again."

"You realize you're breaking the law by doing this, right?" I had to get Thibodeaux back to some kind of rationality before he did something stupid and started to fight.

"That's not all I'll break, you rat-fucker."

I spoke to Carter. "You know how much legal trouble you're in? And if he attacks me, you'll both be in jail."

"Be worth it to see your ass get kicked," said Carter.

"I doubt that," I said. "There'll be a civil suit, too, and I could use the money, after someone burned my dojo."

"That's another thing," said Thibodeaux. "The fucking cops came and questioned me about that. You lied to me and then sicced the cops on me."

"You've attacked me, you've made threats, and you've probably attacked my dojo before," I said. "That was you that threw the rock through my window, right?"

Thibodeaux's face went slack, as if he realized he was in too deep. "That wasn't me," he mumbled.

"Right. So you're surprised after making all these threats that the police would want to talk to you. Just like you made threats against Ben, and then got outraged that they'd question you about his death. If you go through life threatening people, then you shouldn't be surprised when the police get involved."

"I didn't have any trouble like this before you came to town," Thibodeaux's voice was almost a wail.

"Yeah, people were afraid of you. But I'm not, and you can't handle that."

"I can handle it. And I can handle you." Thibodeaux slammed his hands into my chest, pushing me back.

"Don't do that again."

Thibodeaux smiled. "Afraid of me, ain't you, you fuck? You know I'd kick your ass."

Actually, I wanted to fight, but I had a bag of thousands of dollars at my feet, and I was afraid of what would happen if Thibodeaux and I got into it. "You attack me again, I'll file assault and battery charges."

"Don't worry," came Carter's voice. "I'll arrange the photos to make it look like he threw the first punch. Go ahead and kick his fuckin' ass."

"Hear that, asshole?" Thibodeaux smiled. "I can fuck you up because I got a witness that says you attacked me."

"What you got," came a voice, "is a pair of handcuffs and a cell waiting for you if you make another move." A man stepped out from the hallway between buildings.

Thibodeaux quivered with rage. "Who the fuck are you?"

"Detective Sergeant Raymond Lagasse," said the cop, showing his badge. He pointed a finger at Carter, who was trying to melt away. "Don't you move, either, asshole, or you'll be in the cell next to him."

"Uh, Sergeant, I never thought I'd say this, but I'm happy to see you," I said. "How'd you happen to be coming by?" Though Lagasse had forestalled the fight, now I had the problem of standing on top of a bag of illicit cash, talking to a cop who didn't like me. If he found out what was in the bag, I was in a world of trouble. So I wasn't able to relax, even with the cavalry on the scene.

"Being the shit magnet you are, with death threats, arson, and then this asshole muttering how he was going to get even with you, I figured I'd stop in, maybe increase my arrest stats." Lagasse looked at Thibodeaux with disgust. "Yeah, that's right, dipshit. When you talk about getting even, around cops who can hear, we take notice. After Johnson questioned you, he told me you seemed about to go ballistic. And here you are." Lagasse turned back to Carter. "Hand over the camera."

"He broke my last one," said Carter.

"And I'll break this one if you don't do what I say."

Carter passed Lagasse the camera. "I'll file a complaint."

"You do that, asshole. Right after I book you," Lagasse said. "This is now evidence. We'll hold on to it until the investigation is done."

"What investigation?"

"Seems like you two had a conspiracy going, for starters."

"All I did was ask him where this fuck lived," interjected Thibodeaux. "He wrote that shit in the paper, so I figured he'd know. He told me, and I said I was going to fuck him up, and he said he wanted to come along and watch."

Lagasse beamed. "And just like that, they throw themselves into the fire. Okay then," Lagasse pulled out a set of handcuffs and spoke to Thibodeaux. "Turn around and put your hands behind you."

"You're arresting me?"

"Duh. Can't have you going around assaulting citizens, even this guy." Lagasse read Thibodeaux his rights, and if I hadn't been about to explode with worry, I'd have really enjoyed watching Thibodeaux get what he deserved.

When he finished, Lagasse pulled out another set of cuffs out and waved them at Carter. "Come here. Your turn."

"Are those really necessary?" Carter said, looking appalled.

"They are when I say they are. And I'm saying it." Lagasse cuffed Carter while reading him his rights. Before he led them away, he turned to me. "Do you think you can avoid getting killed for an hour while I book these clowns?"

"I'll see what I can do," I said, striving for nonchalance. But as soon as Lagasse had stepped away, I clutched my bag and ran upstairs to my apartment. I didn't breathe until I had the door securely locked behind me.

CHAPTER 38

A thudding startled me awake. Someone was pounding on the door to my apartment, and my heart was now trying to match the beat. The clock said two in the morning, and anyone at your door at that time of night isn't bringing you good news. And if they do it when you're babysitting a bag of illicit cash, you expect the worst. I tried to reassure myself that if someone had been after the money, they'd have just kicked the door in.

I'd had a hell of a time figuring out a hiding place, and settled for the storage closet at the end of the hall, a locked room that rarely got used. Using another skill from my unsavory past, I'd picked the lock, and stuffed the bag of cash behind the mop buckets, pails, and a carpet vacuum.

The pounding continued.

"Yeah, yeah, I'm coming," I yelled at the door. I pulled on a pair of pants and put on the shirt I'd worn all day, and padded out to the front. "Who is it?" I stood to the side, not directly in front of the door. Some bad guys just shoot straight through a closed door, since a lot of people stand there when answering.

"Police. Open up."

"Lagasse? Is that you?"

"*Sergeant* Lagasse. Open the fucking door."

I opened the door, and Lagasse stood there with a uniformed officer.

"What do you want?" I wondered what was going on now.

"Do you know a Wade LaPierre?"

I couldn't really lie about it. "Yeah."

"He was found dead, outside your burned-out dojo."

Oh, shit.

"Get dressed. We've got some questions for you down at the station."

"I'm still half-asleep and liable to say anything, so I'm calling my attorney."

Lagasse looked grim. "That would be a very good idea."

When the cops confirm that you should call your lawyer, you're in a world of shit. I don't know how he did it, but less than half an hour after I made the call, Gordon Parker strode into the interrogation room in a three-piece suit, looking fresh and awake. His flaming red hair was groomed and his eyes showed he was ready for battle. He might be terribly expensive, but in cases like this, I was certainly glad to have him working for me.

For once, I'd kept my mouth shut and refused to talk at all until Parker arrived, except to ask for coffee, which they had graciously provided. I shook with Parker, and he turned to Lagasse.

"Sergeant, please fill me in on why you dragged my client out of bed in the middle of the night."

"Another acquaintance of his was murdered tonight. A drug dealer by the name of Wade LaPierre."

Parker went on. "And this couldn't wait until morning because ..."

"Because the deceased was found outside the recently arson-stricken business of Mr. Taylor," Lagasse replied. "And in a homicide, minutes count. And considering Mr. Taylor's violent past with persons in Mr. LaPierre's profession, we thought we should chat. I am sorry for the

196

inconvenience," Lagasse smiled like he wasn't sorry at all, then yawned. "I had to get up for this myself."

"Your apology and your dedication are noted, Sergeant," Parker said. "May I have a minute in private with my client to confer on how he may know the deceased?"

Lagasse nodded for the uniform to leave the room with him, and Parker and I were alone. I launched into a quick account of finding out about LaPierre's business on the set, and how I'd been told to back off, but how I'd followed him.

"You followed him, after you assaulted him," Parker rubbed his forehead. "You do love getting yourself into trouble, don't you? How did you find out where he lived?"

I swallowed. "A friend had someone run down the license plate."

Parker tsked. "You realize they're probably going to find that out, and whoever gave out that information is in trouble. This is a homicide investigation, and everything will be examined." Somehow it had been great to have Thibodeaux get in trouble for doing it, but when it was turned around on me, it wasn't funny anymore. I might have cost someone their job and pension.

"It gets worse." I explained about cutting the lock at the storage facility and entering the unit, but I didn't say anything about the money.

"Jesus," said Parker. "Breaking and entering on the property of a murder victim. Lovely, just lovely." He saw the look on my face. "But you were right to tell me. If that clerk sees the lock on that unit and makes a report, it'll probably get connected. You signed your name, right? Anyway, the clerk would have a description, and they'll eventually connect you. So we've got that working against us too. Anything else?"

"Well, I didn't kill him."

"Praise be, we've got that going for us. Where were you all night?"

"Well, Sergeant Lagasse arrested a couple of guys at my place just after five, when one came after me."

Parker sat back and shook his head. "Unbelievable. Tell me about this part."

I ran through how Thibodeaux had come to my place, and how Lagasse had been on the spot to stop him from attacking me.

Parker made some notes. "And then you stayed in until they came for you? Alone, I take it?"

"Yeah."

"Anything incriminating at your place? Because if I know Lagasse, he's probably got a warrant on the way."

The blood drained from my face.

"What is it?" Parker now looked weary.

I had to work up some spit to talk. "A big bag of money."

Parker stared at me for a moment, and then burst out laughing. I didn't see anything funny, but he went on laughing. Then he noted my silence and got control. "Wait, let me guess at how perfect this is. That money was somehow connected to the deceased."

I nodded, and he laughed again. "You stupid fuck, how are you not in jail?"

I put my head in my hands, knowing that the cops had a good motive for charging me with LaPierre's murder. I didn't think they knew I'd actually been following LaPierre, or I'd have been arrested already. But they were putting the pieces together, and they had enough to pin it on me. If they found the money, there was no way I could stay out of jail. My greed had got me thoroughly screwed, and my only hope was that they might not get that far.

Parker spoke again. "He mentioned you had a past with drug dealers. I know some of it, but tell me more."

"Last year, I beat up a pusher in the men's room at Denny's in Lewiston. They never charged me with anything, but they kind of knew it was me."

"And all that business with the drug ring." said Parker, musing. "Yeah, with a pusher dead, they're going to go after you full-bore, unless we can give them something or somebody else. You know," he paused. "If you keep going around assaulting people, you're going to wind up behind bars."

The irony was not lost on me, as I'd said something similar to Thibodeaux earlier in the day. The law was definitely a two-edged sword, and it looked like it might cut me once again.

"So who would kill someone to get you into trouble?"

"Maybe the same guy who burned my dojo. Ollie Southern, most likely." Parker scribbled the name in a notebook. "I had a run-in with a Japanese gangster named Oto on the movie set, maybe he could have done it. Thibodeaux's crazy enough, if they released him. I don't know if Stone is that over the edge."

"Stone?"

"Richard Stone, the developer."

Parker shook his head again. "You make the most interesting enemies."

I sighed.

"Anything else you want to tell me before he comes back? Any other crimes around Portland that could tie you to this LaPierre?"

I shook my head. There was a knock at the door. Parker called out. "Come in."

Lagasse and the uniform entered. Lagasse sat at the table, across from us.

"So Counselor, is your client ready to confess?"

Parker smiled. "Innocent men shouldn't confess, Sergeant. We want to help you find the real killer."

"We're working on that. I take it your client has no objection to our search warrant for his living space, such as it is?"

"No objection at all," said Parker. I was glad he'd warned me about this, or I might have reacted and made Lagasse even more suspicious. Search warrants were specific, and I doubted they'd have authority to check other rooms than mine. I hoped not, because my life depended on it.

"And how about a DNA test?"

Parker raised an eyebrow. "If it will help exonerate my client, we'll cooperate fully. You found something on the victim, I take it?"

"Maybe," said Lagasse, watching me closely.

"That's great," I said. "It's not mine, so that'll put me in the clear."

"We'll see," said Lagasse. "Where'd you go last night after I left you?"

"Nowhere. Up to my apartment, and stayed there until you woke me."

"Where'd you go for dinner?"

"I microwaved a meal and ate in."

"Nobody can confirm where you were?"

"I live alone."

Lagasse leaned forward. "You admit you had a beef with this LaPierre?"

"Yeah, but I didn't kill him. And if I did, it would be pretty stupid to dump his body at my dojo. That screams frame."

"Who would want to frame you?"

"You arrested two of them earlier."

Lagasse leaned back again. "They were both in Holding. Unless they're magicians, and slipped out past the front desk and the cameras, I don't think it was either of them."

"But they both made phone calls, right?" Parker cut in.

"Yeah, we're running that down," Lagasse admitted.

"You admit the possibility that either could have called someone to do it."

"Save it for the courtroom, Counselor."

"I just don't want you convincing yourself that my client did it. You know he has dangerous enemies."

Lagasse tapped a pen on the table. "You laying this at Ollie Southern's door?"

"Who better?" I spread my hands. "You know he's out there, just waiting."

"He's on our list," said Lagasse. "Anybody else you want to throw under the bus?"

"Same list as my dojo getting burned. How about a hardcore gangster named Oto, works out on the movie? He's Yakuza."

"Tell me why he'd want to do something like this."

"I made him, and we had some words. He lost some serious face. I doubt he'd forget that. He convinced them to take over my job, and he was there when I brought LaPierre to the director, who said to cut him loose."

"And you didn't like that. You've got a thing for pushers."

"I didn't kill him, though."

"So who put the hurt on you?" Lagasse indicated my bandage. He switched gears suddenly, trying to confuse me.

"Accident," I said.

"Somebody defending themselves by accident?"

"Happened yesterday, so don't get your hopes up. Ask the emergency room doc at Maine Medical."

"Okay, back to your list of enemies," said Lagasse. "Anyone you want to add to it?"

"You've got a convicted killer and a gangster. That's a good place to start."

Dale T. Phillips

CHAPTER 39

I was so sure that a smiling Lagasse was going to come back in the room to arrest me for the murder of LaPierre that I couldn't believe it when the cops finally let me go. Outside the station, I breathed in the cold, crisp morning air, and almost wept for joy, however short-lived my freedom might be.

Parker joined me, looking like a disappointed father. His red hair glowed in the morning sunrise. "You know, they may still come back and arrest you," he said. "They just don't have enough right now. But they're working to get it."

"I know. But if the killer's DNA is on the victim, maybe that will be enough."

"That would be an excellent turn of events."

"I'm going to call J.C. and tell him his friend on the police force that got me the address off the plate number is in big trouble. I'll pay for your services if the guy needs you."

Parker nodded. "I'll say goodbye now, but given your propensity to get into trouble, I'll probably be seeing you before long. Oh, and by the way, my son says thank you."

"For what?"

"You're putting him through Harvard." Parker looked around. "Can I give you a lift?"

"How much will that cost?"

Parker smiled. "No charge."

We didn't say anything on the short ride back to my apartment. I ran up the stairs, and saw a book of matches sticking in the doorjamb. In a hurry, I pulled them free and opened the door. It was obvious the place had been searched, as things had been moved around and left out of the cupboards and drawers. Small as the room was, it couldn't have taken them long.

Saying a silent prayer, I moved down the hall and once more picked the lock on the storage closet. I dug down in back, and the bag was still there. Hardly daring to breathe, I pulled it out. It still had weight. I took it back to my room and opened it, and saw the welcome sight of the sweet green money. Chunks and chunks of it. I pulled a few out, marveling that it was still here.

I sat there on the kitchenette floor and almost sobbed with relief. I'd escaped disaster by the narrowest of margins. I hugged the bag, and patted it, despite the fact that it had almost been my downfall.

The question was, what to do with it? I had a safe-deposit box, but what if the police got a warrant to search it? If they found a huge pile of cash, I'd be cooked. I was so paranoid, no hiding place was safe enough.

I took the bag back outside and locked it in my car trunk. I drove to a convenience store with a pay phone outside. It was early, but J.C. was an early riser.

"Morning," I said.

J.C. sounded awake enough. "Let me guess. Bail money?"

"Almost. Gordon Parker was with me, so they didn't charge me yet."

"Good God, I was kidding. What is it this time?"

"Someone killed a drug dealer from the movie shoot and dumped him by my dojo. So they dragged me out of bed and questioned me, but they didn't have any evidence to charge me."

J.C. sighed. "Some people go their entire lives with less trouble than you find in a day."

"I need a favor. That safe of yours. Do you have room in it for a couple of gym bags?"

"Do I want to know?"

"You do not."

"Wonderful. Sure, bring over whatever package you've got, as long as it's not part of a body or something."

"Aw, come on. In that case, I'd tell you to lend me a shovel."

"Since you're coming out this way, you better show up with doughnuts and gourmet coffee."

"The place on Congress?"

"Of course."

When J.C. opened the door, I handed him the doughnuts and takeout coffee cup. He took them, grunted, and stood back to let me in. I'd stopped off at a sporting goods store and bought two gym bags, and transferred the money. I hefted the two bags and carried them in. J.C. led the way down the hall to his study. The safe was there, and the door was open. I went to it and slid each bag in. I gently closed the safe door and heard the click as the lock engaged. Then I started breathing again.

J.C. was happily working on one of the doughnuts.

"Thanks," I said. I held the original bag the money had come in. "And can you get rid of this?"

He eyed me. "Anything else?"

"Yeah, your friend that ran down that license plate for me. Since the guy was killed, they'll probably track that. He could get into some hot water. I'll pay for Gordon to represent him, if he needs it. Sorry. I had no idea this would happen."

"You never do," J.C. said. He looked sad and pissed off at the same time.

I left, too embarrassed to say anything else. As I drove, I got to wondering about the money. Was that the reason LaPierre was killed? Had he found out it was gone and told somebody? Probably not, unless he'd made another run back to the storage place.

That got me thinking about the cut padlock on LaPierre's unit, because after he found out he'd been ripped off, it wouldn't have mattered. But his murder changed everything. If they discovered the cut lock on his unit, the management would report it, and the police would likely eventually tie it to me. But without a report, the cops might not find out about the unit, since a pusher hiding drug money probably wouldn't rent the place using his real name.

Maybe the management had already found it, but then again, maybe they hadn't. I wanted to know. I stopped by a hardware store and bought a padlock, and drove out to Westbrook. I went in the storage facility lot, parked, and walked along the units.

The cut padlock was still there. You probably wouldn't notice it unless you were looking for it. I tore open the packaging on the new padlock, and used a handkerchief to handle it. I removed the cut lock and substituted the new one, being careful not to leave any fingerprints. I snapped it shut, feeling like that was the end of my troubles with LaPierre.

Now completely fried, I went back to my apartment. I was ready to catch the rest of my sleep from the night before. I pulled the matches out of my pocket, feeling horror envelop me.

The logo on the matchbook was *Harley Davidson Motorcycles.*

Ollie Southern, my stalker. He didn't ride a Harley, but he was a biker, and the message was clear. The matches meant he'd burned my dojo, and was letting me know it. Coming in right after the cops showed that he'd been watching, and wasn't afraid of them. He'd make his move regardless of them. It was an act of bravado, meant to scare me. And it worked. In my state, I wasn't about to try to sleep here, knowing he could be watching, waiting to kill me. I made a quick call to Lieutenant McClaren to let him know, but had to leave a message. I may have sounded a bit panicked.

Quickly packing an overnight bag with a few things, I got back out to my car, looking all around. I was so spooked I even got on the ground and looked underneath, in case he'd planted a bomb. There was nothing. I turned the key in the ignition, and didn't blow up.

I drove around until I was sure I wasn't being followed, and found a cheap motel out by the Maine Mall. Only when I was safe behind a locked door with a chair wedged under the doorknob and the curtains drawn did I feel safe. I took a warm shower to calm down, and finally collapsed into bed.

Dale T. Phillips

CHAPTER 40

My rest was haunted by nightmares and ghosts. After a few hours of fitful sleep, I woke in the afternoon, groggy and wondering where I was. The previous day seemed like another bad dream. I took a cold shower to wake up, and thought about my next move. Ollie had been watching where I lived, stalking me, and he'd probably burned down my dojo. Had he seen me following LaPierre, and killed him to try and pin it on me? Or was it Oto, or even someone else? No, it had to be someone connected to me, because they'd dumped the body outside my dojo, tying me in to the murder. Had they known I was following LaPierre, or it was just a happy coincidence for them?

I checked out of the room and stopped for something to eat. Then I went to the hospital to look up Samantha. I walked into her room, but an elderly woman was in the bed.

"Sorry," I said. "Wrong room." I backed out and checked the room number. It was the correct one, so they must have moved Samantha. I stopped by the nurses' station to ask about her.

"She left," came a familiar voice behind me.

"Hey there," I said to Allison.

"She didn't tell you? She checked out."

I was at a loss for words.

Her face twitched, like she was trying not to smile. "Didn't even say goodbye, huh?"

"Well, I told her we wouldn't work out, because I was still carrying a torch for someone."

That put a crimp in Allison's *schadenfreude*. "Sorry."

"Yeah, me too. I felt responsible for her getting hurt."

"You always do, even when it's not your fault." She put a hand on my arm. "How are you making out?"

"Terrible." I felt like telling her about almost getting arrested for murder, but decided that was a bad idea.

"I miss you," she said suddenly.

"Nice to know," I said. "I sure miss you."

"I have to get back," she said. "Call me sometime."

She left, and I stood there wondering if her words meant something more. But between Samantha and Allison, I was completely ignorant of how women thought and why they did what they did.

But there were more important things going on. I needed information, and wanted to speak to Harada. Probably my best way to get through was to talk to Ponytail or Spiky-hair, so I drove out to the Deering Oaks shoot and asked around, but they weren't there. Next I went to the warehouse site, and found them talking with the second-unit director. When the director moved off, I sidled up to them. They didn't look happy. In fact, no one on site did. Ponytail stripped off the wrapper from a pack of cigarettes.

"Hey guys, what's up?"

Ponytail looked at me. "Did you kill him?"

"Who? The drug dealer? No. But someone tried to make it look like I did. You think I kill people?"

Ponytail shrugged. "We wouldn't be making this film if you hadn't."

He had a point, but I wasn't happy about being reminded of it. "Is that why you're looking so sour? Because the supply chain has been disrupted?"

Ponytail made a sound of disgust. "That's bad enough, but we lost another few hours of shooting. Goddamn fire."

"There was another 'accident'?"

"Yeah, small one. It got contained, but fucked up our schedule again."

"Maybe they'll believe me now when I say someone's sabotaging the shoot."

"No shit, Sherlock." Ponytail crumpled the cigarette-pack wrapper in his fist. "I'd like to find the fuck who's doing it. We're supposed to have security here."

I smiled. "Where's Oto?

"How the hell should I know?"

"He's the security guy, remember? The one they replaced me with."

"And I thought you were the only fuckup."

I smiled again. "I want to talk to Harada again. Can you arrange it?"

Ponytail looked down at the cigarette pack and licked his lips. "Why should we?"

"Maybe I can help stop whoever's doing this, so you guys can get back to filming."

"How's that worked for us so far?"

"Just put me in touch with him. Let him make the call."

Ponytail took a cigarette from the pack and studied it.

"How long have you quit for?" I said.

"Two years, three months, twelve days," said Ponytail. "But the way this week has gone, I really fucking want one."

"And I want a drink," I said. "And yeah, it would taste great, but then I'm back on that roller-coaster again, and can't get off. Don't do it."

Ponytail looked at me. Spiky-hair reached over and plucked the cigarette from Ponytail's hand and broke it in half. Ponytail looked at him. "What'd you do that for?"

"He's right," said Spiky-hair. "Shit's bad for you. You don't want to start again."

"Goddamn the both of you," Ponytail said, hurling the pack into a wastebasket as he stalked off.

We watched him go. "We'll call Harada," said Spiky-hair. "You wait here."

"One more thing," I said. "Samantha, the production assistant that got hurt doing Janelle's stunt. She checked out of the hospital. She still around?"

"We took her to the airport about two hours ago." Spiky-hair looked at me with something like pity. "Didn't say anything, huh? Sorry, but that's how it is in L-A. When we're done with somebody, we're outta there."

I sighed. "Not very considerate."

"Consideration gets you killed in our business. You show your feelings, you get eaten alive."

I looked at him. "This is the most I've heard you talk since we met."

He shrugged. "Too many in our biz shoot their mouth off and get into trouble. The more I keep my mouth shut, the less shit I have to swim through."

"I wish I could do that. You're a lot smarter than me."

Spiky-hair just smiled.

CHAPTER 41

Ponytail came back a few minutes later. "He'll talk to you."

I followed him out to the black SUV and got inside, where Spiky-hair handed me a satellite phone.

I spoke into the receiver. "Mr. Harada?"

"Mr. Taylor."

"Is our deal still on?"

"Of course it is. Why do you ask?"

"A couple of reasons. One, I'd like to run a background check on all your help, especially those on the meal crews, and question them."

"That won't be necessary. I personally screen each man before he is hired."

"Including Oto?"

"Why do you ask?"

"Because someone killed a drug dealer here in town to set me up. Oto is a likely candidate."

"I can assure you, I had nothing to do with that. I'm afraid he no longer takes direction from me."

"He quit?"

"In a manner of speaking. He worked *with* me, but he never really worked *for* me."

Let me guess. He was sent by your Yakuza buddies to keep an eye on things."

"Mr. Taylor, that is not a term we Japanese like to hear. You Westerners think every Japanese businessman is a Yakuza, especially when we get the better of you in a deal."

"I suppose we do think of murderous goons like Oto in a prejudicial light."

Silence on the other end.

"Is that how you got the talent so cheap? Thirty million isn't big budget, but you've got some top names in the biz. What kind of leverage did you use? Blackmail?"

"Another ugly word, Mr. Taylor. Let us say that people of their nature take certain paths in their profession. If they wish to continue on those paths, they do special favors for me."

"So was Oto's job to help you, or stop you?"

"I fear he may have been the instrument of death of my assistant, Kenishi-san, who was loyal to me. It may well be that Oto also killed that drug dealer to frame you, as well as further hamper my movie."

"On orders from the syndicate back home?"

"My associates did not like the idea of the film," said Harada. "But they tolerated it as long as the other streams of income were flowing."

"So what happened?"

"There were some ... irregularities in our dealings."

"You were skimming?"

"Nothing so simple."

I thought about it, and added up what I'd learned. "Let me guess. You were actually competing with them in some areas. Like substituting cheap sea urchins for more expensive ones. And Oto did some digging, and found out."

There was a pause on the line. "You continue to surprise me, Mr. Taylor."

I looked out the window. "So what do we do about Oto?"

"I'm afraid my associates seem to have parted ways with me. They dislike loose ends, so his next move may be to remove me from the board."

"Good thing you have all that protection, then."

"Yes, I believe I am quite safe here. I have worked to make it so. But what sort of protection do you have?"

"What do you mean?"

"If you know enough about my business, that means Oto knows enough about you. And you are another loose end. I do not know which of us he may attempt to kill first, but if I am well-protected, he may try to eliminate you while he bides his time waiting for me to show myself."

I rubbed a hand across my face. "I already have another killer coming after me. Maybe they'll fight over who gets to do me in."

"It is not a joking matter. Oto is rather skilled."

"Still kind of tough for a Japanese man to hide out in Maine if the police are looking for him. I'll call them when I'm done talking with you."

"I wish them success in capturing him. But I have no confidence in their ability to do so."

"What is he, a ghost?"

"More like a shadow. He has evaded capture by the Japanese police on a number of occasions."

I did some more thinking. "When you hired me, you anticipated this, didn't you? I wondered why you were so intent on having me on the set. You were always looking ahead. You knew they'd send someone, and you wanted me around as a distraction for him. To take the heat off you. Then while he's hunting and killing me, it gives you some breathing room. And maybe he even gets caught after killing me. You're using me like a chess pawn."

"In the game of go, we also have the concept of sacrificing stones to gain a superior position." Harada chuckled. "Perhaps if you survive, you could come work for me. With Kenishi gone, I could use a man with your skills."

I laughed. "You just confirmed that you put my life up as bait, and you want me to work for you?"

"You seem like a professional who does not hold a grudge when there is no malice."

"It might be too dangerous, working for you when the boys back home don't want you in business anymore."

"Given time, I can perhaps smooth things over. There are ways of making it worth their while to let me alone. But I find this Oto to be a problem. I have thirty million dollars tied up in this film, and he is in the way. I would pay you rather well to make this problem go away."

"Kill him, you mean." I shook my head.

"Whatever is necessary."

"Still pulling strings. I have to hand it to you, Harada-san, you certainly do love to play."

"What else is there, Mr. Taylor?"

"Offhand, I can think of quite a few things."

"Perhaps we are different, then. But as I say, you have your uses. Please do your utmost to keep Oto from stopping the film. After all, you have a financial stake in the success as well, now that you have been reassured that our deal is still in effect."

"I'll see what I can do."

CHAPTER 42

When darkness fell, I went hunting for clues. First, I had to sneak onto the warehouse lot to see what I could find out about their recent fire. Ralph the security guard was on duty, but he stayed in his little shed. With his nose buried in a magazine, it proved to be easy to slip past him, just like Theo had said.

The warehouse door was locked, and the high windows gave out a dim light from inside. The windows were up far enough that I couldn't reach them to get in, so it looked like a little lock-picking was in order. Keeping one eye open for the security guard, I used my Swiss Army knife and a paperclip. My rudimentary skills were quite rusty, and the lock pins kept slipping when I almost had them in place. I was exposed out here, and I had that feeling of being watched, so I kept turning my head to make sure Ralph didn't emerge from his guard shack across the lot. It took me almost fifteen minutes to finally work the last of the pins and get the thing open. I cracked the door just wide enough to slip inside.

There was some damaged canvas where the fire had burned a backdrop, but I couldn't tell anything in the nature of a clue from the remains. I looked up at the catwalk overhead, figuring I'd climb up and survey the whole place, to get a perspective. I was about to do just that when the door opened and closed.

I looked to see who had entered, expecting Ralph, and hoped I could talk my way out of this one. A chain rattled as Oto clicked a padlock shut, securing the door. He turned and stared at me. He removed his suit jacket, then his shirt, then his pants, folding them neatly and putting them to the side. An icy hand seemed to grip the back of my neck, as I realized he didn't want to mess up his clothes when he killed me.

The fact that he didn't seem worried that I'd run out the side door indicated he'd probably blocked it from the outside before coming in. And I didn't think Ralph would come and rescue me, even if Oto hadn't killed him already.

Oto's body looked as solid as carved blocks of wood, and he was tattooed from his neck to his wrists, and all the way down to his ankles. Hardcore, life-long Yakuza gangster, and he'd likely done prison time in some of the deadliest incarceration joints humans could create.

He grinned, cocking a thumb at his chest, to the Japanese character for the number five. He pointed at me, and held up six fingers. He'd killed five men, and I was going to be next. This wasn't a duel of honor, it was an execution.

I had no illusions. As a fighter, I was a decent club scrapper, but this guy had been born into a fight club where to lose was to die. I'd killed by accident, but wasn't a killer. It's a hard thing to do, and it takes a special kind of wiring to deliberately take a human life with your bare hands. Most people just couldn't do it. That's why we have so many guns, because it makes killing easier. But the man at the door would be trained in every dirty trick in the book, and when he got his hands on me, I was dead.

I ducked behind a set, desperate for a weapon. His bare feet slapping on the floor echoed as he ran after me. I grabbed the sides of a mirror and threw it as he came in range. He swatted it away in a shattering explosion. I hurled a flowerpot filled with dirt, then two lamps, but they bounced off him with no apparent effect. I pushed a table in his way, which he flipped out of his path like a child's toy. I ran around the set, desperately looking for some place of safety, death at my heels.

Running all the while, I found I'd circled back to where I'd been when he first came in. I saw the broken shards of mirror, and had enough sense to reach down for a sliver. I also grabbed a handful of flowerpot dirt with my right hand. I palmed the mirror shard in my left, leaving only a corner sticking out past my thumb and forefinger. I made two fists and turned to crouch in a fighting stance, as Oto came around the corner, barreling towards me.

I threw a punch with my right, opening my hand to hurl the dirt at his face. He closed his eyes, and my left shot out. He bobbed his head sideways to avoid what seemed like a face jab, but my improvised shiv tore into the flesh at his neck, my real target. His eyes went wide, and his hand clapped to the wound, already blossoming with fast-flowing blood. Now if I could just stay alive and moving, he might bleed enough to weaken.

I ran, pulling chairs behind me into his path. One chair was by the ladder to the catwalk, and I used that as a springboard, jumping onto the ladder to scramble up. Anything to get his heart pumping the blood faster, and keep his hands too busy to cover his wound.

He was right on my tail as I made it onto the catwalk. He was just a few steps behind me when I grabbed the rail and vaulted over. I'll bet that surprised him.

Arms outstretched, I landed on the stunt pad, slapping downward with my arms to absorb the impact. I rolled, tumbling over the edge. I stumbled to the floor, but regained my footing, and heard him hit the pad above me. I ran back to the props and sets, grabbing and throwing anything and everything within reach. It may have looked like a screwball comedy scene, but it was like being pursued by a Terminator.

I gripped a prop painting and turned back toward him. He came at me, covered in his own blood, like a demon from hell. Spearing quick, short jabs with the corner, I held him off for a few seconds, until he smashed it away. I leaped back and tipped over a fake wall piece. He swatted it aside, and I sent another at him, and then another. Each one slowed him down by a precious second or two. I grabbed a chair, and held the legs toward him like I was a lion tamer. He had to grip it to wrestle it away. I pushed off hard and grabbed another chair, and we did the same dance. It took him a little longer to get this one from me. I ran again. He had slowed, but was still following. It was a grim game of Keep-away.

We came to the open space, and I stopped as he rushed to grab me. A beat before he reached, I dropped into a backward Aikido roll, coming up in fighting stance. He lunged at me, but I did another roll, and then another, always changing direction, making him expend energy to keep up. My dropping away made me hard to grab or hit, and Oto couldn't just recklessly charge, because I'd always come up ready for a counterattack.

I started to get light-headed, but he was coming in slower, and I knew he was tiring. He stumbled, and on my next time up, I fired a jab that caught him by surprise, before I rolled away once more. The next time he moved in quicker, and hit me with a couple of shots that jarred me. He got hold of my shirt, then it tore as I pulled away. I kicked at his knee and connected, as his downward block felt like it almost broke my leg. I kicked again, but lower, cracking his shin, while I fired a spear thrust to his face. He blocked my hand and grabbed my arm. For a second, I saw my own death, but I twisted, and his bloody hand lost its grip. If he'd been fresh, I'd have been dead already, but a tired fighter reacts more slowly.

I'd recovered my balance and rolled away from his next charge. He lunged when I came up, but I simply backpedaled. He followed me for a few steps and stopped.

220

His eyes had a faraway look as he sank to his knees. From about twelve feet away, I watched as the last of his life ebbed from his body. He finished bleeding to death before me, but his warrior code would not even let him fall. He died on his knees, as all expression drained from his face, and his head sank onto his chest.

Heart pounding, I tried to get my breathing and vision back to normal. I was alive. The demon had run his course, and I felt the adrenaline surge subside in me. Giving his body a wide berth, I made my shaky way to the door. I searched his discarded clothes and found the key. Trembling, I unlocked the padlock and stepped out into the cool night air. I breathed it in, and thought it had never tasted so good.

Dale T. Phillips

CHAPTER 43

The police put me in another interrogation room. This was becoming a bad habit. At least I'd stopped shaking.

Gordon Parker came in, looked at me with what I took to be dismay, and I tried to crack a joke. "We've got to stop meeting like this."

Parker shook his head and sat down. He opened his briefcase, took out a legal pad and tossed it on the table in front of him. He removed a pen, clicked it, and got ready to write. "So what is it this time?"

"Ask Lieutenant McClaren. I spoke with Harada earlier tonight, and he told me Oto was on the warpath. He also asked me to keep an eye on the set. I was there when Oto came in to try and kill me. He almost succeeded."

Parker sat back. "What time did you talk with Harada?"

"Late afternoon. The movie people can confirm. I called on their satellite phone. Why?"

"He's dead."

"What?" I stared at him.

"He was shot sometime just after sunset, apparently through a window, from what I heard. The assailant got away."

"That was Oto."

"Who then came to kill you. And happened to find you on the movie set, illegally trespassing."

"Harada asked me to keep watch there," I protested.

"The now deceased Mr. Harada, who can neither confirm nor deny your claim."

"Hey, whose side are you on?"

"Be glad I'm on yours. Maine didn't have too many homicides until you came along, so the police are frothing at the mouth. Sergeant Lagasse would love to put you away."

"For killing a Yakuza in self-defense?"

"For finding you with another dead man. One you admit you killed."

"Oto was probably the one who killed Kenishi, and LaPierre too."

"The police will say it's rather convenient that the person you claim killed everybody is the one you slew."

"He was sent by the mob back in Japan to keep watch on Harada, who was pulling a fast one by switching cheap sea urchins for the more expensive stuff. Oto got wind of it, and started messing with Harada's plans. I just got in the way, so he killed LaPierre to try to pin it on me. It didn't work, so he came after me, once he'd killed Harada."

Parker sat back and studied me. "What in God's name made you get involved with these people?"

"I didn't want to," I said. "But they kept insisting."

"Hell of a mess," Parker said. There was a knock at the door. "Come in," said Parker.

Lieutenant McClaren entered, followed by Lagasse. I looked at their faces to see if I could get a clue as to their state of mind, but they gave nothing away.

McClaren sat down, while Lagasse leaned against the wall and crossed his arms.

"So, tell me a story," said McClaren, and I went over what I'd told Parker.

McClaren tapped a pen on the table. "We found a Japanese fisherman in the water down by the docks. He'd been killed from a blow to the side of the neck and dumped in the harbor."

I thought about it. "Oto had dealt with the crew of the Japanese boat. He probably hired one of them to take him out to Harada's island and back. Then he killed the guy to cover his tracks, and came after me."

"Busy man. Lot of killing in two days."

"He's a professional button man from Japan. That symbol on his chest means he's killed five men with his bare hands."

McClaren looked impressed. "And you survived."

"Not by much," I said.

"No indeed. Want to see a replay?"

"What do you mean?"

"With all those accidents on the set, they put up security cameras and didn't tell anyone. Your death match was recorded."

"Jesus," I said. "Did you see it?"

"I did. You are one lucky cowpoke."

"So you believe me, then."

"The evidence bears it out, but we're going to test you for gunshot residue anyway, just to take that part of it off the table."

"Sure," I said. "Good. You won't find any on me, but you will on Oto. He probably tossed the rifle into the harbor on the way back. And he was the one sabotaging the movie set, too, to mess with Harada."

"All tied up with a bow, then," said Lagasse. "Except for one dead pusher."

"Get those lab results back, and you'll probably see it's Oto's DNA. It certainly isn't mine."

"Got yourself a good lawyer and a good story, with a dead guy to take all the blame. So you think you're going to skate again."

"Is there something you're going to charge me with, Sergeant?"

"Soon as I can. You know a Ronald Cushman?"

"No. Should I?"

"He's the guy who lost his job running down a license plate for you, asshole. Chew on that."

"Sergeant, why don't you take a break?" McClaren's voice was calm, but there was steel in it.

Lagasse left, and McClaren looked at me as if his gaze could burn right through me. "If you ever try to get anybody on the force to do something like that again, we will charge you."

"I asked somebody, and they asked somebody else. I'm sorry, I didn't know. They fired him?"

"Early retirement."

I looked at Parker, who coughed. "He's sixty-one, so he was due soon anyway. He gets to keep his pension."

"Thank you," I said.

McClaren spoke. "Sergeant Lagasse's been friends with him a long time. He's pissed at you for getting his friend canned. You'd better walk a straight line from now on."

"I've still got Ollie on my tail."

"We're keeping an eye out, but if he was smart, he's faded back into the woodwork until the heat dies down. But he'll be back. Give any thought to leaving, like I suggested?"

I shook my head. "No, Lieutenant, I'm staying right here. This crazy shit has got to stop sometime."

"Not with you, it doesn't."

CHAPTER 44

The following day, I drove out to Fort Williams. Most of the movie equipment was gone: the trailers, trucks, lights and sets, and with them, the crowds. It reminded me of a Ray Bradbury book, *Something Wicked This Way Comes*, where a dark carnival appears on the edge of town to work evil magic, and then just as suddenly vanishes one morning.

I saw a familiar figure watching a crew of men load a trailer truck. "Hey Theo," I said.

"Look at you, alive and all," he said, and smiled at me.

"You had your doubts?"

"News has been talking about a lot of dead people."

"Yeah. Oto got that little pusher, and then Harada. Killed a fisherman, too, and tried to get me."

"But you a hard man to put down."

"So far, at least," I said. "So with Harada dead, they figured, game over, huh?"

"Something like that. Man ain't writin' no more checks."

"Will you miss them?"

"Won't miss the bullshit," Theo said. "Hours and pay were okay, though. Scenery was pretty good, too. Speaking of which, what happened to your lady friend?"

"She up and left without saying goodbye."

Theo gave me a look. "You're a damn fool, you know that?"

"Yeah."

"So what are you going to do now?"

I shrugged. "No idea. I'm just happy to still be alive and out of jail. The last two days have been a little intense."

Theo laughed. "That's what happens when you jump into a meat grinder."

I started to protest, then realized where I was. This was the place where I'd decided to make a stand against a group of killers. I'd survived, but it had been my choice to risk everything.

"Guess you're right," I said. "Take it easy, huh?"

"See you around."

I left this place of death and bad memories, and drove back to Portland, stopping by Deering Oaks, but everything from the movie set was gone. The park was as it had been before the movies came to town, all traces of intrusion gone.

I stopped at a good Mexican restaurant, where J.C. met me for lunch.

"Sorry again about your friend," I said. "Did you know he was a good buddy of Lagasse's?"

"Ron should have retired two years ago," said J.C. "He'll be all right. But now you've burned one of my important contacts. So you're buying today."

"Crazy how it all turned out. I lost a hundred grand and my chance to open my dojo."

"So what will you do now?"

"I don't know. I'd like to stay out of the police station for a time. Let me tell you, having Gordon there was a big help."

"I guess with what you've got tucked away in my safe you'll be able to afford his services."

"Yeah," I said. "Things worked out in one area, at least. And I can help Ron out, too."

"He should be all right, but I'll ask. A couple of grand for a fishing boat might be a good way to make it up. So you're out of the movie business?"

"God, they're nuts. They were all over me when they wanted me to sign on, and then they're gone, without any goodbyes." I thought about Ponytail and Spiky-hair, Janelle and her entourage, Claude Conway and his goofy, good-buddy act, the angry fight coordinator, Taggart, the pissed-off director, and most of all, Samantha. "I wonder if they'll think back on this time, or if they'll want to forget it as that failed project."

"Doesn't seem to be a lot of self-reflection in that crowd," said J.C.

"You're right there. It's funny," I said. "Everyone goes back to what they were doing before, like it never happened, except me."

J.C. looked at me. "And the dead men. You get to rise from the ashes, like a phoenix. But they're gone, with all their plans and schemes and future. You still get to have one, if you want."

"Yeah. I just don't know what it'll be."

"You'll think of something."

"And Ollie's still out there somewhere."

"Memento mori. Knowing you'll die someday makes you do more now, savor it."

"Well, sure, but I could really do without a killer stalking me."

Things might have gone back to normal for some, but for me, everything was still whirling. Shadows of the past still haunted me, affecting my life and how I reacted. I envied those who didn't carry around Death's baggage everywhere they went. I was like Jacob Marley in *A Christmas Carol*, forging my own burdensome chain and hauling it with me.

"Enough moping," said J.C. "I can't stand morose company. It's all just shadows, you know. Like Plato's cave. We see the reflection, and think it's real. Like the movies. Just shadows on a wall."

"Are you getting all intellectual on me?"

"Wait until I start talking about Jung and his concept of shadows."

"Can it wait until I finish my burrito?"

"Philistine. I was just trying to distract you from your self-pity."

"I guess I just need a fresh start to my fresh start."

"Some people never learn," said J.C., shaking his head.

CHAPTER 45

Every morning since I'd escaped death, I got up early so I could watch the sun rise. I wanted, needed even, to see each new day begin, when I'd come so close to never seeing another one.

I went out to Fort Williams and slipped in, even though it wasn't officially open yet. I sat on the rocks, jacket zipped up against the morning chill from the sea, and watched the relentless waves pound against the shore. But I was still here. I may have lost just about everything, but I was still kicking, and grateful to be so.

I thought about all the craziness and death that had happened. But it had not come from this place, it had come from outsiders, from those who did not belong. People like myself. Or rather, not like me. They came and did their thing, dumped their trash, and left. But I stayed, because this area was still a healing place, at least for me. It wasn't some flickering shadow, like so many of the places I'd lived. It had substance, and it called to me, as it had once many years before.

No, Ollie wouldn't drive me away. Nor would Thibodeaux and his anger, Mason Carter and his incessant newspaper stories, or Stone and his boycott and Fire Marshal buddy. I'd remain, and keep trying to build something of value. Whatever that was.

The sun peeked up over the horizon, and the water below changed color rapidly. The shadows receded, and the morning began. It was a new day indeed.

I spent a few hours down at Back Cove, taking the long walk around, watching the joggers, dog-walkers, and even a few windsurfers. People seemed to be having fun, enjoying life. I still had a giant hole in me.

It was early afternoon, sunny and warm, when I made my way over to the strip mall where my dojo had been. I parked and got out, looking at the charred ruins of my dream. I didn't have the heart to try again. I sat on the hood of my car and just stared at the blackness, feeling my own darkness inside. I truly didn't know what else to do with my life from here on out. I was glad I was alive, but I didn't know what to do.

A vehicle pulled up next to me. Allison got out of her car. "Hey," she said.

"Hey," I replied.

She looked at the wreckage for a minute, then at me. "Scoot over."

I moved to the right side of the hood, and she jumped up beside me. We sat in silence awhile.

She turned to me. "Sucks, huh?"

"Sure does," I said.

"But you almost died in there before."

"It was part of a life I was trying to build, along with you. I wanted something to show I could change, that everything wasn't about going out to get killed. For the first time in my life, I was trying to be responsible. And now ..." I felt I might lose it. She was so close, and yet not with me.

She sighed. "Sometimes you care too much about the wrong damned things."

I nodded, and we sat for a while longer. Some minutes later, she reached over and took my hand. "Want to go get an ice cream?" I looked at her. She smiled. The real smile, the one that I fell in love with. The one filled with promise.

And just like that, spring was back, and hope flooded back into my soul. The blackness in my world evaporated like a shadow in the light.

THE END

LIKE MORE ZACK TAYLOR?

Sign up for my newsletter to get discounts on upcoming titles

OR- Get a free ebook or audio book

At http://www.daletphillips.com

A CERTAIN SLANT OF LIGHT

Trapped by a final promise to a dying woman, a reluctant Zack Taylor seeks her missing grandson, a slippery con-man of the art world. Zack discovers the corruption beneath the glossy exteriors, confronting murder, greed, fraud, and a host of crimes that belie the beauty of the art in which the people deal.

Read on for the exciting first chapter in *A Certain Slant of Light*, the fourth book of the Zack Taylor series.

CHAPTER 1

A deathbed request is one you don't refuse. So I didn't, though not liking it one bit. I'd flown from Maine down here to Miami because she'd asked me to. She being Mrs. Harris, my former landlady who'd become my friend.

As I made my way through the hospital corridors, I heard the squeak of the nurses' shoes as they made their rounds, and smelled the cleaning fluids that tried to mask the other odors that came with sickness and death. I hated hospitals in the first place, as people I'd loved had died in places like this sterile tomb. In addition, I'd been forced to spend too much time in them recovering from the effects of my stupidity and bad choices.

The sunshine streaming through the window illuminated the dying woman in the bed, enveloping her in a halo of white light. I hesitated at the door of the room, not seeing any movement of her frail form. If she was sleeping, I didn't want to wake her.

Silently edging closer, I could see only the slightest rise and fall to indicate she was still breathing. The ravages of cancer had left little resemblance to the strong, vibrant woman I'd said goodbye to just the year before. A certain slant of light beamed upon her, and Emily Dickinson's words about that came to mind. The Belle of Amherst had written about visitations from Death, and here was a woman who would soon find out for herself. Swallowing, I couldn't rid myself of the lump in my throat.

Her eyelids fluttered open, and she gave me a weak smile. "Zack." Her voice was like the rustle of dry paper. She looked as if she'd been squeezed like an orange, all of life's juices gone. Tubes snaked from her in different directions, modern medicine keeping her in this world. It didn't seem like a mercy.

I gently touched her on the tips of her fingers. "Hey there."

She reached to grip my hand as if afraid I'd run away. "Must ask you for a promise."

"You have to tell me one thing first."

"What?"

I smiled. "All the time I've known you, I never knew your first name. Just Mrs. Harris."

"Rita," she whispered. "It's short for Marguerite."

"That means 'Little Pearl'."

"Yes."

"And Mr. Harris?"

"I was with Hal twenty-two years. I'll be seeing him soon." She closed her eyes and sighed. When she opened

236

them again, they had tears in them. "But I need to know something before I go."

"What's that?"

"Where my grandson Steven is. I need you to find him."

"You've lost touch?"

"Some time back, he suddenly came to see me. He hadn't been by for a while. He wanted the Dali, the one you like, that's hanging in my living room. It's genuine. Worth a bit. He needed money and wanted to take it."

"And you said no."

"He'd have just sold it. I gave him some money, but he was angry I wouldn't give him the painting. I haven't heard from him since."

"Any idea where he is?"

"There's a card in the drawer." She gestured to the stand beside the bed.

I opened the drawer and took out a business card. "Sheldon Rabinowitz." I looked at her. "Good Irish name."

She smiled. A weak one, but a smile nonetheless. "He'll explain everything."

"What do I do when I find Steven?"

"Bring him here. He'll come, since there's some money from my estate. Late, but better than never."

"Does he get the Dali, too?"

"No. For you."

"Me?"

"You always loved it. You'll take care of it, not just sell if off for cash. I want it protected. It has great sentimental value."

"You met him, didn't you?"

"Salvador? Oh, yes. He was something, I can tell you that. A true artist, but such a joker. It was after the war, when people were getting back into life and art. A fun crowd back then. Quite an experience." She had a faraway look, remembering places of long ago. "I had so many interesting experiences. Now, nobody will know or care."

"I care," I said. "I can stay here, and you can tell me about them."

"No. You have to go find Steven. I need to see him before I go. Promise me you'll bring him back in time for me to see him."

I hesitated. I didn't want to say I could do something when I might not be able to make it happen. What if I couldn't find him in time? What if he didn't want to come back? What if he was dead, or in jail? But in the end, when someone you care about is looking at the end of life, you tell them whatever they want to hear. "I promise," I finally said.

"Good, good." She closed her eyes, then slowly opened them. "Find him, Zack. And hurry. I don't know how long I can last."

AFTERWORD

A Shadow on the Wall is the third in the series about Zack Taylor, a man with many problems. He struggles to do better, but the shadows of his past weigh him down. When he tries to help others, he finds that doing good is a complicated matter, and unintended consequences force life-changing alterations.

The shadows haunting this book are many, and those familiar with the work of Carl Jung will see how deep they go. Additionally, the theme draws on the idea of Plato's cave, with the concept of people seeing only a distorted reflection of reality. There is much to think about for those who wish to peel back the layers. If not, just enjoy a cracking action yarn.

Should you notice a lack of cell phones and certain modern items, it's because this book is set in the 1990's. There was indeed a booming business in sea urchins off the coast of Maine for a short time, so certain ideas have a basis in reality. But this is a work of fiction, and any resemblance to actual persons, living or dead, is purely coincidental.

Dale T. Phillips

ABOUT THE AUTHOR

A lifelong student of mysteries, Maine, and the martial arts, Dale T. Phillips has combined all of these into A Memory of Grief. His travels and background allow him to paint a compelling picture of Zack Taylor, a man with a mission, but one at odds with himself and his new environment.

A longtime follower of mystery fiction, the author has crafted a hero in the mold of Travis McGee, Doc Ford, and John Cain, a moral man at heart who finds himself faced with difficult choices in a dangerous world. But Maine is different from the mean, big-city streets of New York, Boston, or L.A., and Zack must learn quickly if he is to survive.

Dale studied writing with Stephen King, and has published novels, over 30 short stories, collections, as well as poetry, articles, and non-fiction. He has appeared on stage, television, and in an independent feature film, *Throg*. He has also appeared on two nationally televised quiz shows, *Jeopardy* and *Think Twice*. He co-wrote and acted in The Nine, a short political satire film. He has traveled to all 50 states, Mexico, Canada, and through Europe. He enjoys competitive sports, historical re-enactment, and his family.

Connect Online:
Website: http://www.daletphillips.com
Blog: http://daletphillips@blogspot.com
Twitter: DalePhillips2

Try these other works by Dale T. Phillips

Shadow of the Wendigo (Supernatural Thriller)

Dale T. Phillips

The Zack Taylor Mystery Series
A Memory of Grief
A Fall From Grace
A Shadow on the Wall

Story Collections
Fables and Fantasies (Fantasy)
Crooked Paths (Mystery/Crime)
Strange Tales (Magic Realism, Paranormal)
Apocalypse Tango (Science Fiction)
Halls of Horror (Horror)
Jumble Sale (Mixed Genres)
The Big Book of Genre Stories (Different Genres)

Non-fiction Career Help
How to Improve Your Interviewing Skills

With Other Authors
Insanity Tales
Rogue Wave: Best New England Crime Stories 2015

Sign up for my newsletter to get special offers
http://www.daletphillips.com